D1625092

the adventures of
SOPHIE MOUSE

A New Friend

By Poppy Green • Illustrated by Jennifer A. Bell

LITTLE SIMON

New York   London   Toronto   Sydney   New Delhi

LITTLE SIMON

An imprint of Simon & Schuster Children's Publishing Division
1230 Avenue of the Americas, New York, New York 10020
This Little Simon hardcover edition May 2016 • *A New Friend*, *The Emerald Berries*, *Forget-Me-Not Lake*, and *Looking for Winston* copyright © 2015 by Simon & Schuster, Inc. All rights reserved, including the right of reproduction in whole or in part in any form. LITTLE SIMON is a registered trademark of Simon & Schuster, Inc., and associated colophon is a trademark of Simon & Schuster, Inc. For information about special discounts for bulk purchases, please contact Simon & Schuster Special Sales at 1-866-506-1949 or business@simonandschuster.com. The Simon & Schuster Speakers Bureau can bring authors to your live event. For more information or to book an event contact the Simon & Schuster Speakers Bureau at 1-866-248-3049 or visit our website at www.simonspeakers.com.
Designed by Laura Roode
The text of this book was set in Usherwood.
Manufactured in the United States of America 0416 FFG
10 9 8 7 6 5 4 3 2 1
Library of Congress Control Number 2015959776
ISBN 978-1-4814-7601-0
ISBN 978-1-4814-2834-7 (*A New Friend* eBook)
ISBN 978-1-4814-2837-8 (*The Emerald Berries* eBook)
ISBN 978-1-4814-3002-9 (*Forget-Me-Not Lake* eBook)
ISBN 978-1-4814-3005-0 (*Looking for Winston* eBook)

These titles were previously published individually
in hardcover and paperback by Little Simon.

Table of Contents

the adventures of
SOPHIE MOUSE
A New Friend

Contents

chapter 1

Spring Has Sprung!

Buzz, buzz, buzzzzzzz. Outside the Mouse family's cottage, a bumblebee zipped from flower to flower.

Sitting at her easel in the sunshine, Sophie Mouse put down her paintbrush. Her eyes followed the bee. *Oh, to be able to fly,* she thought. *I could see every inch of Silverlake Forest—maybe even to the other*

side of Forget-Me-Not Lake! I wonder how fast a bee flies when he
really gets going. What would it be
like to fly to the schoolhouse for
the first day of school tomorrow?
What would—

"Sophie? Sophie!" Her father's voice called out, snapping her out of her daydream. He was in the doorway of their cottage, which was nestled in between the roots of an oak tree. "Are you done with your chores?" George Mouse asked. "When you are, you can go see Mom at the bakery. She's

making nutmeg popovers today!"

Sophie's little nose twitched. She was sure she could already smell the sweet scent. Nutmeg popovers were one of her mother's specialties. At her bakery in Pine Needle Grove, Lily Mouse surely would have started making the batter at dawn, before Sophie was even awake.

Sophie hated to stop painting. It was the first spring day warm

enough to paint outside! But she had
a little sweeping to do if she wanted
to go to the bakery.

Sophie hurried inside and found the willow-twig broom. She had already swept the three small bedrooms upstairs. Just the main floor was left: under the toadstool table and birch-branch stools, and around the spun-silk couch. Sophie swept all the corners of the kitchen.

Then she swept the pile of leaf bits and dust right out the front door.

"Dad! I'm finished!" she called. "I'm going by Hattie's house on the way to the bakery!" Hattie Frog was Sophie's best friend.

Just then, way back in the rear of the cottage, a mouse's head popped up through a hole in the floor. It was Sophie's little brother, Winston. He was cleaning up the root cellar. "I want to come too!" Winston called.

Sophie sighed. Winston was six. She had been stuck inside the cottage with him for most of the winter

vacation. Now that the weather was warming up, he wanted to tag along with Sophie *everywhere*. "Have *you* finished your chores?" Mr. Mouse asked Sophie's brother.

There was a long silence. When Winston answered, his voice was quiet. "Not yet."

"Well, finish up, then," Mr. Mouse replied. "You and I can go later."

Sophie leaned her broom against the wall by the front door. Then she was off with an extra spring in her step.

It wasn't that Sophie didn't like her brother. They had fun playing together. But Sophie *was* two years older. And it was the very last day of vacation. She wanted to fill it with eight-year-old adventures! Halfway to the stream, Sophie heard a rustle in the tall reeds to her right. She stopped in her tracks.

"Hello? Is someone there?" Sophie called out.

She perked up her ears, listening carefully. But all was silent and still.

Sophie's eyes scanned the reeds.

She thought she could just make out a shadowy shape among them. She squinted and took a step closer.

Now Sophie was sure: Someone was in there.

But who was it?

— chapter 2 —

A Perfect Day

"Harriet Frog!" Sophie called, using Hattie's full name. "Is that you in there?"

There was no answer from the reeds. So Sophie called again. "It's me—*Sophie!*"

There was a rustle. The reeds parted slowly. A green eye peeked out. Then Hattie hopped out into the open. "Phew, it *is* you," Hattie said. "I heard footsteps coming and—well, I'm glad it's you!"

Hattie was shy around strangers. But not with Sophie. They had known each other for as long as they could remember.

Sophie told Hattie about the pop-overs. "Want to come to the bakery?" Sophie asked. "We could stop at the lake on the way!"

Hattie giggled and shook her head. "Uh, Sophie. Forget-Me-Not Lake isn't exactly *on the way*."

Hattie is always so practical,

thought Sophie. But she was right. The lake was a bit of a hike. "Well," said Sophie, "we have lots of time. And it's our last day of vacation!"

Hattie smiled. "I'll tell my mom!" she cried, then hopped off toward home. Sophie followed and waited outside Hattie's house. It was built on the bank of the stream, not far from

Sophie's. Half the house sat floating on lily pads, right on the water. The other half was built into the pebbly bank. Sophie knew that her dad, the town architect, had helped Mr. and Mrs. Frog design it.

Soon Hattie was back and she and Sophie were running off toward the lake. "Please be home before dark!" Mrs. Frog called after them.

The girls never got into too much trouble in Silverlake Forest. Now and then, Sophie came home with prickers on her tail or muddy clothing. One time she got lost exploring a mole tunnel. But she just asked one of the moles for directions, and soon found her way home.

The path to Forget-Me-Not Lake was long, winding, and lined with berry bushes.

"Oh, these make the best purple paint!" Sophie exclaimed, pointing to some ripe berries. She stopped to gather some. Sophie carried pouches in her pockets at all times—for exactly this reason. Both the pouches and Sophie's pockets were always stained with berry juice.

Finally, the girls arrived at Forget-Me-Not Lake. The water glittered in the morning sun.

Sophie looked at Hattie. "Are you thinking what I'm thinking?" she asked.

"Well," Hattie said with a smile, "you do have one wild imagination,

Sophie Mouse. But if you're thinking we should go lily-pad hopping . . . hop on!"

Sophie climbed onto Hattie's back and held on tight. Hattie leaped out onto the lake. She jumped from lily pad to lily pad, hopscotching across the water. This was their very favorite thing to do at the lake.

Later, the girls made flower crowns.

They looked for four-leaf clovers. As usual, they didn't find any.

They skipped stones on the water, counting the jumps.

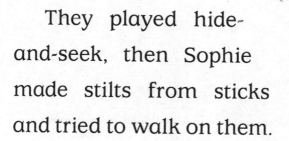

They played hide-
and-seek, then Sophie
made stilts from sticks
and tried to walk on them.

When their tummies
grumbled, it was time for popovers.

The bell on the bakery door jingled
as they entered. Mrs. Mouse was at
the counter. Several animals were

waiting patiently in line.

Sophie and Hattie scurried behind the counter just as they always did. Lily Mouse took a moment to hug them. Then she whispered, "A fresh batch of popovers just came out. Help yourselves."

The girls smiled gleefully and hurried back into the kitchen.

As they nibbled their popovers, Sophie sighed happily. It was turning out to be a great last day of vacation. Already she was thinking about the picture she would paint about it. She'd be sure to use her new purple berry paint!

chapter 3

School Surprise

The next morning, dressed in her best jumper dress and leggings, Sophie hurried to get her backpack ready. She was eager to see friends she hadn't seen all winter. *Plus,* she thought, *you never know exactly what will happen on a first day of school!*

Sophie zipped up her backpack.

"Bye, Dad!"
Sophie called as
she hurried out the door.

"Wait for me!" Winston
cried. He ran out after her, his shoe-
laces still untied.

Sophie had almost forgotten:
Winston was starting school this
year! Mrs. Wise's one-room school,
Silverlake Elementary, was for all
students ages six to ten.

Sophie bent down to tie Winston's shoes. "Mrs. Wise will want you to learn to tie these yourself," she said firmly. Then, in a gentler voice, she added, "Come on. I'll show you the *fun* way to school."

Instead of taking the path into Pine Needle Grove—past the bakery, the library, and the post office—Sophie led Winston to a little-known trail. It cut behind the library and ran through a tunnel of honeysuckle branches. The flower buds were just

opening. Sophie could hear Winston
behind her, taking deep breaths of
the scent.

The trail came out in the school-
yard. Sophie led Winston up to the
front door and inside the pine-bough
schoolhouse.

"Sophie!" Hattie's voice rang out. Sophie turned and waved. Hattie was standing with her big sister, Lydie, and their friend Ellie the squirrel. Just then, Piper the hummingbird and Zoe the bluebird flew in through the

windows. Willy the toad was already sitting at a desk next to Malcolm the mole.

And Ben the rabbit and his little brother, James, entered the room behind Sophie and Winston. Winston

knew James from preschool. So they
went off to find two desks together—
a mouse-size one for Winston and a
bigger one for James.

Sophie headed over to say hello to
Hattie, Lydie, and Ellie. But just then,
Mrs. Wise, a neatly dressed owl with
glasses, stood up at the front of the

room. "Class!" she said. "Please take your seats!"

Sophie hurried to get a maple-bark desk by a window so she could see outside. She loved looking out the window— even if Mrs. Wise *did* catch her daydreaming sometimes.

"Welcome back to school!" said Mrs. Wise when the students were seated. "I'm happy to see you all bright-eyed and ready to start

another season. Now, I think we're all here—" Mrs. Wise counted the students. "Oh! We're missing our *new* student. His family has just moved to Pine Needle Grove. His name is Owen. I know you will all make him feel very welcome."

At that moment, the door creaked open.

"Here he is now!" said Mrs. Wise. "Welcome, Owen."

All the students turned in their

seats—and gasped. Ellie and Malcolm both let out little squeaks. Ben's ears stood straight up. Sophie rubbed her eyes to make sure she was seeing this right.

Owen was . . . a *snake*?!

First-Day Jitters

Sophie glanced at Hattie, who was sitting behind her. Their eyes met. Sophie could tell that Hattie was just as nervous and surprised as she was.

A real snake . . . in real life! Sophie thought. She'd never seen one before. She bet none of her class-mates had, either.

"Come in, Owen," Mrs. Wise said

to him warmly. "Find a seat."

Everyone watched as Owen respectfully took off his brimmed cap. Then he slithered up the center

aisle. He passed up an empty desk next to Sophie's. She breathed a sigh of relief. She didn't want to be rude, but she didn't know if she wanted Owen to sit next to her, either.

Some of Sophie's ideas about snakes came from books. But most had come from stories—spooky stories that older animals told about

poisonous sea snakes or hissing ghost snakes. Surely they couldn't be true . . . could they?

Owen found a desk in an empty row. Mrs. Wise began the math lesson. Other students took out their notebooks.

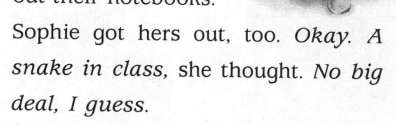

Sophie got hers out, too. *Okay. A snake in class,* she thought. *No big deal, I guess.*

Then, during quiet reading time, Sophie heard a *"Pssst."* She looked up. Owen was leaning toward Zoe's desk, which was in front of his. He was trying to get her attention. But Zoe was lost in her book.

Owen said *"Pssssst,"* a little louder. Zoe didn't hear.

Owen tried one more time. *"Pssssssst,"* he said loudly. Startled, Zoe fluttered up and out of her seat, turning to glare at Owen.

"Why are you hissing at me?" she demanded.

Owen cleared his throat. "Your bookmark is on the floor," he said. His voice was a little raspy, but gentle.

Zoe picked up her bookmark and sat down. "Oh," she said quietly. "Thanks."

At recess, Owen passed by the swing set and accidentally swatted the swing James was on with the end of his tail. The swing went flying way too high.

"Whooooaaaa!" James cried out. "Help me!" he shouted.

James's brother, Ben, hurried over to help him down. As he did, Ben snapped at Owen, "You need to be more careful!"

Owen looked very embarrassed. "Sorry," he said quietly. "It was an accident." He slithered over to a bench and coiled up, all alone.

Sophie saw it all from across the yard. She was playing hopscotch with Hattie, Lydie, and Willy. "Hey!" Sophie said to them. "Should we ask Owen to play?"

Willy shrugged, but said nothing. Lydie didn't seem so sure. "Can snakes even hop?" she asked.

Hattie patted Sophie on the back. "I think it's a good idea," she said. "But I'm afraid to ask him. *You* ask him."

Sophie took a deep breath. She started walking over to the bench.

Then Owen looked up and saw her coming. Sophie lost her nerve and turned around.

Silly Sophie! she scolded herself. *Why are you so nervous?*

She tried to work up the courage to try again. But before she could, recess was over and it was time to go inside.

After school, Sophie and Winston got ready to walk home together. "So what did you think of school?" Sophie asked her brother as they walked out the door.

Winston replied excitedly, "It's so fun! I get to sit next to James. I get my

very own desk. I like Mrs. Wise. . . ."

Winston went on, but Sophie didn't hear the rest. Outside the schoolhouse, she saw Owen being greeted by another snake—probably his mom.

Sophie imagined that Owen's mom was asking Owen about *his* day at school.

And Owen did not look happy at all.

— chapter 5 —

Snake Stories

At dinner that night, Winston told Mr. and Mrs. Mouse about the new student.

"Wow, a snake for a classmate?" Mrs. Mouse exclaimed.

Sophie nodded. "Malcolm said that snakes can be sneaky," she began.

"And Ben said they're scary!" Winston added.

"And quick-tempered," said Sophie. "At least, that's what Piper told us."

Mrs. Mouse seemed surprised at their words as she passed the cheese biscuits. "Actually," she said calmly, "I was *going* to say: 'A snake for a

classmate? How *delightful*.'"

"Delightful?!" Sophie and Winston cried in surprise.

Mr. Mouse nodded. "Have you or any of your friends ever *met* a snake before?" he asked.

Sophie and Winston shook their heads.

Mr. Mouse smiled. "Well, *I* have," he said. "Your mother and I used to know a very nice snake."

"Yes," agreed Mrs. Mouse. "And I thought you two knew better than to make up your mind before you even get to know someone."

All of a sudden, Sophie's biscuit didn't taste so good. She thought again about Owen sitting alone at recess, and how sad he looked after school. Now she really, *really* wished she had asked Owen to play.

Later that evening, Sophie went to find her dad. George Mouse was at his design desk, working on a blueprint for a shrew family's new house.

"Dad?" Sophie said. "Would you

tell me more about the snake you and Mom knew?"

Mr. Mouse put down his pencil. He turned to look at Sophie, smiled, and ruffled the fur on her head. "Her name was Olivia," he began. "Her family lived near here when your mom and I were young. We'd play together all the time—especially over in the buttercup patch. Then, one day, when I was maybe ten, she and her family moved away. I missed her a lot. Your mom did, too."

Sophie was quiet for a moment, then she said, "Sounds like she was a very good friend of yours."

Mr. Mouse nodded. "She *was* a very good friend," he said.

Sophie shuffled to her room. She got into her pajamas, climbed into her bed, pulled up her quilt made of milkweed fluff, and turned off the light.

As she lay in the dark, Sophie made a decision.

Owen was brave enough to walk into a school full of strangers, she thought. *Tomorrow, I can be brave enough to ask him to play.*

chapter 6

Time Flies When You're Having Fun!

At school the next day, the first thing Sophie did was look for Owen. But he wasn't there.

The students took their seats. Mrs. Wise called attendance. They started their lesson.

Still no Owen.

Sophie looked back at the door many times during the day. At every rustle or creak or whoosh of the wind, she turned to see if it was Owen arriving.

But the day flew by, and Owen never appeared.

The same thing happened the next day. Everyone was in school except for Owen. Where was he?

At least it was library day, which took Sophie's mind off of it. She *loved* library day! "Each of you may check out one book this morning," Mrs. Wise told the students.

The following day, the class went on a field trip to the beautiful

Goldmoss Pond. Sophie was so excited that she didn't even notice Owen was still missing.

Before Sophie knew it, the week-end had arrived. On Saturday after-noon, she and Hattie went to help out at the bakery. Mrs. Mouse had a brand-new recipe to try out.

She was known far and wide for her unusual and tasty creations. Today's experiment was a cinnamon-spiced buttercup cake. "If it's not a ten on the Tasty Scale, it's not ready to be sold," Mrs. Mouse told the girls with a wink.

She emptied a basket onto the counter. Two delicate buttercups fell out. "Oh dear," said Mrs. Mouse. "We're definitely going to need more buttercups."

"We'll go pick some!" Sophie suggested. Hattie nodded in agreement.

The buttercup patch was very close to the bakery.

Mrs. Mouse hesitated, then said,

"Okay, but be back in half an hour."

Sophie and Hattie skipped out of the bakery, baskets in hand.

chapter 7

one stuck Mouse

Sophie and Hattie could just see over the tops of the taller flowers. They made their way out into the center of the buttercup patch. Then they looked around in all directions.

"Wow!" said Sophie. "It's like a big yellow ocean of buttercups . . . I think." Neither she nor Hattie had ever been to the ocean. There were

plenty of lakes, ponds, and streams
in Silverlake Forest, but no oceans.
They started picking the smaller

flowers. Sophie grabbed a stem, pulled, and stowed the flower in her basket. *Grab, pick, stow. Grab, pick, stow.* Sophie got into a rhythm. Her basket was soon a quarter full.

"Exactly how many buttercups do you think are in this patch?" Sophie asked Hattie over her shoulder. But Hattie didn't answer. "Hattie?"

Sophie turned. Hattie was off in a different part of the field.

Sophie went on picking. *Could it be a million buttercups?* she wondered. *A billion? Grab, pick,*

stow. Imagine the shade of yellow paint I could make from these! Maybe Mom will let me take home some extras. Buttercup yellow . . . that would be a great color to have, and not just for flower paintings. I could paint amazing sunrises! And sunsets! And cheese and—

"AAAAHHHH!" Sophie was falling! Her basket of buttercups went flying as she slid down a narrow hole in the ground. Just as suddenly, she landed with an *oof!* on the hard dirt floor.

It took a moment for Sophie to clear her head. But she wasn't hurt—just very startled. She stood up and dusted off her dress. Then she looked around. There were no side tunnels, and the top of the hole was way out of reach. She tried to get a grip so she could climb up. But the dirt just crumbled in her hands.

She needed help to get out.

"Hattie!" she called. "Haaaat-tie!"

She held her breath, listening

for Hattie's reply. None came. Now Sophie wished she and Hattie had stuck together. *She's too far away to hear me! How will I ever get out of here? Oh no. Will I be stuck down here . . . forever?*

"HATTIE!" Sophie tried again at the top of her lungs.

Sophie listened—and heard a rustle from above. "Hattie? I'm down here!"

As Sophie looked upward, a head popped into view. It was small and round and wearing a brimmed cap. And it was peering into the hole!

Then a voice called down, "Sophie Mouse? Is that you?" It was a little raspy, but also gentle.

Now Sophie was sure. It definitely wasn't Hattie.

It was Owen!

chapter 8

To the Rescue!

For a minute, Sophie was so surprised, she couldn't speak. Finally,
she squeaked out, "Yes! It's me! I-I
can't get out."

Owen was quiet a moment. Then
he said, "I have an idea. I'll lower my
tail down. Grab on. I'll pull you out!"

"Oh!" Sophie exclaimed. "Okay!"

Owen's head disappeared as he

turned around. He lowered his tail—down, down, down—until it was within Sophie's reach.

For a split second, Sophie hesitated. She was afraid to be down in the hole, alone. But she was afraid to grab on to Owen, too.

Then Sophie remembered how brave Owen had been on the first day of school.

And here he is being brave again, thought Sophie. *It's time for me to be brave, too!*

Sophie grabbed on. She felt her feet lift up off the ground. Inch by

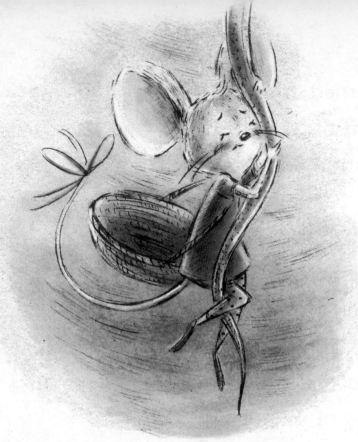

inch, Sophie rose, higher and higher.
She held on tight, trying not to slip,
until she could reach out and grab
onto the lip of the hole. Then she
scrambled up and out, safe at last!

"You saved me!" Sophie exclaimed as she got to her feet. "Thank you!"

"No problem," Owen said bashfully. "It's no big deal."

Gazing out over the buttercup patch, Sophie spotted Hattie off in the distance. Sophie waved, and Hattie came running over.

"I was so worried!" Hattie cried, huffing and puffing. "I turned around and you were gone—" She stopped, catching sight of Owen. "Oh, hi. W-what are you doing here?"

Before Owen could answer, Sophie

burst out, "Owen just saved me! I fell into this hole and he pulled me out!"

Hattie looked into the hole. "Oh my goodness," she said. She gave Sophie a hug. "I'm so glad you're okay." Then she beamed at Owen.

"Way to go, Owen!" she cried. "Quick thinking!"

Owen looked down at the ground. "I don't know . . . I just . . . well, she needed help, so I helped," he said.

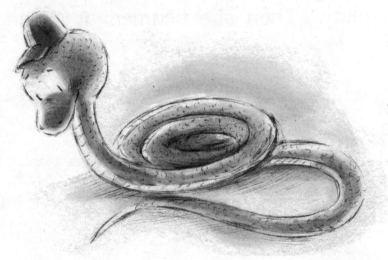

Just then, a voice from behind Sophie and Hattie made them jump. "Oh, here you are!"

Sophie and Hattie turned to see a grown-up snake towering over them. Sophie's heart skipped a beat, and Hattie reached for Sophie's hand.

But then Owen said, "Oh, hi, Mom. This is Sophie Mouse and Hattie Frog."

Looking again, Sophie recognized Owen's mother as the same grown-up who was waiting for him at school on the first day.

"Hello, Sophie. Hello, Hattie," Mrs. Snake said kindly. "Very nice to meet you. I'm Olivia."

Olivia? thought Sophie. *Olivia Snake? Wait a minute. It can't be. Or can it?*

Is she the *Olivia Snake—Mom and Dad's long-lost friend?*

chapter 9

Old Friends and New Friends

"Excuse me, Olivia—I mean, Mrs. Snake," said Sophie. "Did you grow up around here?"

Olivia's eyes went wide in surprise. "How did you guess?" she said with a laugh. "I used to play all the time in this very buttercup patch!"

"With George and Lily Mouse?!" Sophie asked excitedly. A speechless

Olivia Snake nodded, so Sophie added, "They're my mom and dad! My mom is at her bakery, right over there." She pointed toward town. "We were picking buttercups for a recipe she is trying out."

Suddenly, Sophie had a great idea: They could all go back to the bakery together to surprise Mrs. Mouse. Mrs. Snake loved the idea.

Hattie, Owen, and Mrs. Snake helped Sophie pick fresh buttercups to replace the ones that had scattered when she fell. Then they walked together to the bakery. Sophie and

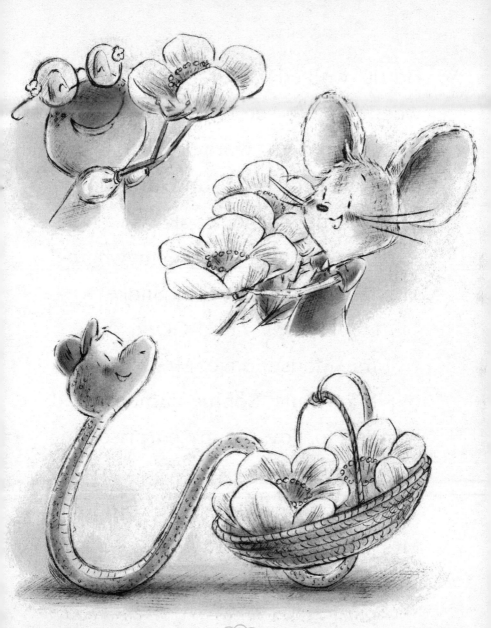

Hattie walked in first. Mrs. Mouse was happy to see them because she had started to worry. Then Olivia and Owen came in—and Mrs. Mouse nearly dropped her cookie sheet.

"Oh, I'd know that face anywhere!" Mrs. Mouse said. "Olivia Snake!"

"Lily Mouse!" cried Olivia.

Mrs. Mouse gave Mrs. Snake a big hug while Sophie jumped and clapped for joy. Happy surprises were the best!

"Well, this calls for a celebration!" Mrs. Mouse declared.

She fixed up a tray of pastries and made a pot of tea. Then the two old friends sat down at a

café table to chat and catch up.

Meanwhile, Sophie, Hattie, and Owen set up their own tea party behind the counter. They took turns sneaking pastries from the grown-ups' tray.

After a few cookies, Sophie asked the question she'd been wondering all week. "Owen, how come you never came back to school?"

Owen hesitated. "Well, my mom used to be a schoolteacher," he said. "She's teaching me at home. For

now, at least." Owen looked down. "Anyway . . . I didn't think anyone liked me."

"Oh, no!" Hattie burst out. "That's not true! Not . . . exactly."

Sophie gulped, feeling embarrassed. "I think it was just, well, we
were all a little nervous. None of us
had ever met a snake before." She
took a deep breath. "We're really
sorry, Owen."

Soon it was time for the Snakes to leave.

Sophie thanked Owen again for saving her.

"Will we see you at school on Monday?" she asked.

Owen moved slowly toward the door. Then he looked back at Sophie.

"Maybe," he said with a smile.

chapter 10

Better Late Than Never

Sophie tapped her pencil on her desk. She stared at the clock on the schoolhouse wall. It was Monday morning. Mrs. Wise was about to start the first lesson.

Owen wasn't there.

Sophie looked over at Hattie, two desks away. They had saved the desk between them for Owen.

"I thought for sure he'd come,"
Sophie whispered to Hattie. She
slumped in her chair. *I guess I was
wrong.*

Just then, the door swung open.
A ray of sunlight fell across the

classroom. Owen hurried in. "Sorry I'm late, Mrs. Wise," he said, out of breath.

Sophie heard some of the students whisper in surprise. But this time it was *Sophie* who squeaked—from happiness.

She waved wildly to Owen. Hattie motioned for him to take the desk between them. He came over and sat down.

"We are so glad you're here!" Sophie whispered to him.

She could feel everyone looking at them—including Mrs. Wise.

Sophie's eyes met her teacher's. Mrs. Wise winked and smiled warmly.

At recess, Sophie and Hattie led Owen outside. "What should we play?" Hattie asked.

Sophie shrugged. "What do you like to do, Owen? Hopscotch?"

Owen shook his head. "I'm not good at jumping," he said. "But I am good at jump *rope*."

"Huh?" said Hattie.

Owen smiled. He rested his head on the end of the bench. He propped up his tail on the base of the seesaw.

Then he twirled his body around and around. . . .

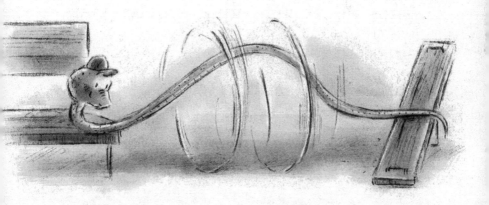

"A jump rope!" Sophie and Hattie cried, laughing.

Sophie hopped in and started singing, "School, school, the golden rule, spell your name and go to school: S-O-P-H-I-E!" She jumped out.

Hattie took her turn: "H-A-T-T-I-E!" She jumped out.

Lydie hopped over and asked if she could play. Then Ellie and Malcolm joined in.

Ben walked up to Owen as he was

twirling. "Doesn't that hurt, Owen?"
Ben asked.

"Nope, not at all!" said Owen. "It's
fun. I'll get tired after a while. But
not yet. Jump in, if you want!"

Ben smiled and jumped in: "B-E-N!"

Before long, the whole class was
playing.

That evening, Sophie painted a picture using her newest color, buttercup yellow. It was a landscape of the buttercup patch under a bright orange and pink sunset. In the corner, she painted a mouse, a frog, and a snake, playing together.

Sophie stepped back and studied her work. She thought it was one of her best yet!

Sophie smiled. She was happy—because of her painting, because Owen had come back to school and everyone liked him, and most of all, because she had made a new friend.

The End

the adventures of
SOPHiE MOUSE

The Emerald Berries

Contents

chapter 1

Forest Friends

In the heart of Silverlake Forest, a mouse, a frog, and a snake talked and played by a stream. It was just another after-school playdate for Sophie Mouse and her good friends, Hattie Frog and Owen Snake.

Owen was lazily draped over a low-hanging tree branch. He watched as Sophie, sitting on a rock below,

drew in her sketchbook. She was
adding a bee to her garden scene.

"That reminds me of our field trip
to see the honeybee hives!" Owen
said. "It was my favorite part of
school this week."

Mrs. Wise, their teacher at Silverlake Elementary, had taken them to see how honey was made by the worker bees.

"Want to know *my* favorite thing from this week?" called Hattie. She was hopping from lily pad to lily pad.

"It was the visit from Mr. Wallace, the flying frog!"

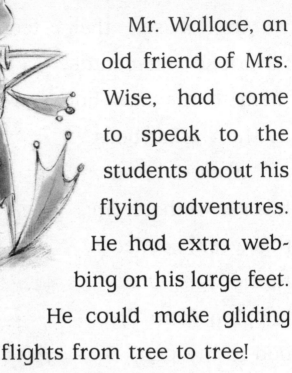

Mr. Wallace, an old friend of Mrs. Wise, had come to speak to the students about his flying adventures. He had extra webbing on his large feet. He could make gliding flights from tree to tree!

Spotting a fish in the clear water, Hattie raced to see if she could beat it to the big rock Sophie was on. "Look at me!" Hattie shouted. "I'm a flying frog!"

Meanwhile, Sophie sketched away, her nose almost touching the paper. She was adding some ants to a log in the foreground. *Maybe one of them should be carrying something,* Sophie thought, *like a seed or a piece of fruit. Ants are so strong!* Sophie

remembered a book she had read once. *It said ants can carry things fifty times heavier than they are. That would be like a mouse carrying a pineapple! I don't think I could carry a pineapple. Plus I don't think I'd want to. The one I saw once in the general store was so prickly looking. . . .*

"Sophie?" Hattie was calling. "Sophie! Hello? Sophie?"

"What?" Sophie replied. She looked up from her drawing. "What did you say?"

Owen and Hattie laughed. "You didn't hear a word we said, did you?" Hattie asked.

Owen added, "I was asking you what *your* favorite part of this week was."

"Oh!" said Sophie. She put her pencil eraser to her chin as she thought it over. "That's easy. Having art class outdoors!"

Mrs. Wise had taught a lesson out-side on Wednesday. It was one part science and one part art. The assign-ment had been to look for different types of mushrooms and draw them.

Sophie loved the outdoors. When she was in school, she liked to sit right next to the schoolhouse window. But Mrs. Wise said it made Sophie too daydreamy. Sophie had to admit: She did love an adventure—even if it was just an imaginary one.

"Haaaar-ri-et!" came a voice from upstream. It was Hattie's mom. She was the only one who called Hattie by her full name. "Anyone over there hungry? I've got a snack for you three!"

Snack? Sophie, Hattie, and Owen looked at one another. Then the race was on to Hattie's house.

— chapter 2 —

A Trip to Town

"Queen me!" Sophie said to her little brother, Winston. They were playing acorn-cap checkers. Sophie already had six queens, while Winston had only two.

It was Saturday morning in the Mouse family's cottage nestled between the roots of an oak tree. Sophie's father, George Mouse, had

lived there all his life. In
fact, his grandfather had
built the cottage and
most of the things inside—
including the checkers set Sophie
and Winston were using.

Winston's whiskers twitched. He
was looking for his next move. He

reached down and double-jumped two of Sophie's pieces.

Sophie gasped in surprise—then laughed. "You're getting better, Winston."

Winston smiled proudly. He was six. That was two years younger

than Sophie, and he was always trying to catch up.

Just then, they heard their mother,
Lily Mouse, calling from outside. "I
have some errands in town! Anyone
want to come?"

Sophie jumped up. "I do!" she cried.

"But we're not done!" Winston complained.

"We'll finish later," Sophie said, and she dashed to the door. "I promise! Don't let Dad take my place!"

Sophie hardly ever passed up a trip into town. It was only a short walk down the path. But it was a fun change from their sleepy corner of Pine Needle Grove. The library was there, as well as the post office, the

bookstore, and Lily Mouse's bakery,
of course.

Today was Lily Mouse's day off,
and she had some things to pick up
at a few of the other shops.

First, she and Sophie stopped at

Little Leaf Bookstore. Sophie loved the smell of brand-new books.

Mrs. Mouse picked up a pastry cookbook she had ordered. She was famous for coming up with her own unique recipes. But she was always looking for new ideas. "Enjoy!" said friendly Mrs. Follet, the store owner.

Next, they stopped at Handy's Hardware. Mr. Handy, an elderly badger, had put aside some wooden pegs that Mr. Mouse needed for a building project.

Then they zipped into the general store. Mrs. Mouse paid for a tin of dandelion tea. It went perfectly with

the rolls and cakes at the bakery, so she always liked to have some on hand.

Finally, Sophie and her mom stepped into a tiny shop called In Stiches. The owner, a bluebird named Mrs. Weaver, was the town's

seamstress. Mrs. Mouse had asked
Mrs. Weaver to make her a new
apron.

"Hello, Lily! Hello, Sophie!" Mrs.
Weaver called out as they entered.
"Be with you in a moment."

Mrs. Weaver was hemming the skirt of a lovely green silk dress on a hanger.

"Wow!" Sophie cried. "What a color!" The fabric was a deep, shimmery green that had flecks of blue sprinkled throughout. It reminded Sophie of the feathers on a mallard duck.

"Isn't it beautiful?" Mrs. Weaver agreed. She fluttered over to them. "That fabric was dyed with the juice from some very special berries."

Berries? Sophie thought. She had never seen a berry that could make

a color like that. And Sophie knew
her berries. She gathered all kinds
to make different colors of paint for
her paintings.

Sophie needed to get her hands
on some of those berries! *If they*

can make a fabric that color, she thought, *just think what a beautiful paint color they could make!*

"Where do these berries grow?" Sophie asked excitedly.

Mrs. Weaver shook her head. "Oh, nowhere around here, dear," she said.

"Emerald berries grow in *only* one place in the whole wide forest. And it's a place you surely would *not* want to go."

Sophie's brow furrowed. "Why not, Mrs. Weaver?" she asked. She couldn't think of anywhere in the forest she wouldn't go to get berries like that.

Well, except maybe one place. It was a place Sophie had only heard of. It was—

"Weedsnag Way," said Mrs. Weaver.

Sophie gulped.

chapter 3

Sophie Makes
a Deal

Carrying their packages, Sophie and her mother strolled home. "I think I'll make some dandelion tea and read my new cookbook when we get back," said Mrs. Mouse. "Would you like some tea too, Sophie?"

But Sophie didn't hear her mom. She couldn't stop thinking about the emerald berries. *Oh, why can't*

*they grow somewhere other than
Weedsnag Way?*

"Sophie?" Lily Mouse said again.

"Hmm?" Sophie said. "Sorry, Mom.
I was just thinking . . . um . . . can
I go over to Hattie's house to play?"

"Oh!" said Mrs. Mouse. "Sure." She
took the wooden pegs
and the apron,

which Sophie had been carrying. "Come home before dinner, okay?"

"Okay!" Sophie called. And she scurried off toward Hattie's house on the stream, while Lily Mouse went on to their cottage.

Sophie *did* want to play with Hattie. She invited Hattie outside to skip stones on the stream. But she also wanted to tell her friend about the emerald berries.

"What?!" Hattie cried when Sophie told her. "Weedsnag Way?" Her eyes went wide with fear.

"*Shhhhhh,*" Sophie said, looking toward Hattie's house. "Keep your voice down. I know, I know. It's supposed to be dark and scary and all that. But I really want to find those berries! We just need—"

"We?" interrupted Hattie. "You want *me* to go too? But Sophie, we don't even know how to get there. And it's not just dark and scary. It's supposed to be dangerous and . . ."

As she trailed off, Hattie threw a stone in the stream. She had stopped short of saying one other thing.

Sophie knew what it was. Everyone had heard the story. A squirrel from Pine Needle Grove had ventured to Weedsnag Way once. He'd never come back—and no one had heard from him since.

"But no one *really* knows what it's like," Sophie pointed out. She threw a stone, then turned to face Hattie. "Remember how everyone at school was scared of Owen at first? It was because of all the stories

they'd heard about snakes. Stories that *weren't true*!" Sophie shrugged. "Maybe Weedsnag Way is not really scary and dangerous at all."

Hattie was quiet for a minute. She threw stone after stone into the

stream. Some of them skipped. Some of them just plunked into the water.

Then she spoke. "Are you going to go there no matter what?" Hattie asked.

Sophie smiled. Hattie knew her so well. "If I can find a map," Sophie said.

Hattie sighed. "Then I'll come. But on one condition: If we run into any danger, we turn back. Deal?"

Sophie rolled her eyes, pretending
not to like Hattie's rule. But secretly,
she was relieved. She knew it was a
good idea.

Sophie jumped up. "Deal!"

chapter 4

The Journey
Begins

Early the next morning, Sophie added
a few more supplies to her sack: a
canteen of water, a sweater, a hat,
and a scarf. Finally, she tucked in a
tin of mint-leaf biscuits. Hattie loved
those.

Then, all dressed, with her sack
on her back, she paused at the front
door of the silent cottage. Everyone

else was still asleep. She didn't *want*
to tell her parents where she was
going. They might say she couldn't
go. But it didn't feel right just leaving.
So Sophie wrote a note:

Went on a long
hike with Hattie.
Be back before
dark.
Sophie

She left it on the table. *It's not the whole truth,* thought Sophie. *But it's most of it.*

Hattie was waiting outside her front door when Sophie arrived. "Ready?" Sophie asked excitedly.

Hattie nodded, but she looked a little nervous.

"Don't worry," Sophie said. "This will be fun! And I have everything we need." She reached into her sack and pulled out a map. "I went to the library yesterday afternoon. I found a map of Weedsnag Way and copied it down."

On her hand-drawn map, Sophie had marked the path in red ink.

Weedsnag Way had a big red *X* on it.

Sophie led the way. Hattie followed, slowly at first. But as they walked through familiar woods, Hattie's pace picked up. Soon they were walking side by side, laughing and chatting.

Then they came to the banks of Forget-Me-Not Lake. Hattie stopped. She gazed out at the lily pads on the water. Sophie knew what she was thinking. Hattie wished that *this* was

their destination instead of Weedsnag Way. The friends loved coming to the lake together to hopscotch across the water on the lily pads. But they didn't have time today.

Sophie picked two honeysuckle
flowers from a nearby bush. She
handed one to Hattie. As they walked,
they sucked the sweet nectar from
the inside.

A little while
later, they heard a high-pitched
voice coming from the branches
above. "Sophie! Hattie!" the voice
called.

Sophie looked up. "Zoe!" she cried.
She saw their friend from school flying down to say hello. "I forgot that
your house is over here!"

"Well," said Zoe, "my flightless
friends hardly ever come over to this
side of the lake! I guess it feels too

far from home. But for us birds, it's just a quick flight into town."

Sophie and Hattie laughed. "I guess you're right!" said Sophie. "But we're going *very* far from home today." She explained that she and Hattie were going to try to find Weedsnag Way. "Want to come with us?"

"Oh! Oh, noooo!" said Zoe, fluttering nervously. "Weedsnag Way? No, thank you, I do *not* want to come."

And off Zoe flew without another word.

chapter 5

What's That Sound?

"She didn't say she'd ever *been* there," Sophie pointed out.

Hattie didn't reply. The two friends walked on quietly through the woods.

Sophie kept checking the map. "There should be a rocky hillside coming up," Sophie said.

Sure enough, they soon passed a

rise with a rocky face on one side.

"Next we should come to a brook with a big log fallen across it," said Sophie.

There, up ahead, was a babbling brook. The girls used the fallen log as a bridge to cross the water. Their

route took them downstream along the brook. After a while, a large stream joined up with the brook. Now it was more like a river. The water got rougher and faster-moving.

Sophie and Hattie continued on through the woods along the

riverbank. Soon Sophie started to hear a sound. It seemed far off, but it was constant, like a gust of wind blowing on and on.

As they walked, Sophie noticed that the sound was getting louder.

Sophie looked at Hattie. "Do you hear that?" she asked.

Hattie nodded. "What is it?"

Sophie didn't know. But she was curious to find out. She sniffed the air, but all she could smell was the water of the river. She hurried on. The sound got louder . . . and louder . . . and louder. Before long, Hattie had to shout to be heard over the roaring sound.

"SOPHIE!" she cried. "I THINK WE SHOULD GO BACK!"

Hattie had stopped walking. Sophie looked toward the sound, then back at Hattie. She didn't want to go on without Hattie. But she *did* want to know what was making that noise! It felt as if they were so close. The roar almost seemed to shake the ground.

In front of them were some tall

reeds that blocked their view of the way ahead.

Sophie scurried forward a few steps. She parted the reeds and poked her head through.

What she saw took her breath away.

"Hattie! Come look!" she shouted. "You have to see this!"

Hattie hopped over. "Oh my . . ." was all she said.

They were gazing out over a roaring waterfall. The rushing water caught the sunlight and glinted as it fell. Two rainbows made a double arc over the misty pool below.

"I've never seen anything so beautiful!" said Hattie. The fear had

left her face. In its place was a huge smile.

"Now *this* is an adventure!" said Sophie.

She pulled out the map to check their position. She studied it for

several moments. "Huh," she said.
"That's funny."

Hattie looked at the map too.
"What's funny?" she asked.

Sophie looked up at Hattie. "It's
just . . ." she began. "The waterfall.
It's nowhere on the map!"

chapter 6

Lost!

Hattie and Sophie backtracked so they could talk without having to shout. Sophie opened her sack. She took out the water and the mint-leaf biscuits. While they nibbled, they looked at the map together.

"You're right," said Hattie at last. "There's no waterfall anywhere on the map." She looked up at Sophie.

"So what do we do now?"

Sophie folded the map. She tucked it back into her sack, along with the water and biscuits. She sniffed the air and looked around. She wasn't really sure which way to go. *But if I tell Hattie that, she'll want to go home,* thought Sophie.

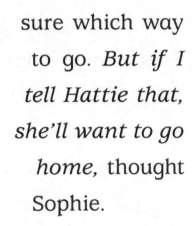

Sophie pointed toward the woods, away from the river. "Let's go this way,"

she said, trying to
sound confident.

Hattie nodded
and followed along.
"Phew!" she said.
"I'm so glad that roar
was coming from a
beautiful waterfall
and not . . . well,
not *something else*!"

They walked and walked, deeper
and deeper into the forest. Sophie
looked up, down, and all around.
She was trying to take everything in.

The trees here are different,

Sophie noticed. She was used to the oak and ash and pine trees in Pine Needle Grove. But these trees were all very tall with smooth, white bark. Hattie seemed to notice too. Now and then, Sophie turned around to find

Hattie studying a tree trunk. The first few times, Sophie didn't think much of it. Then it seemed as if Hattie was stopping more and more. Each time, just as Sophie was about to ask what she was doing, Hattie hurried along to catch up.

"Is it . . . darker here?" Hattie asked after some time had passed. "Or is it just my imagination?"

Sophie looked up. The tall trees and their leaves were blocking out most of the sunshine. "It does seem very . . . *shady*," Sophie said.

They walked on a while longer. A

cold gust of wind blew past. Sophie's
teeth started to chatter.

"Is it *colder* here, too?" Hattie
asked.

Sophie nodded. "That definitely
was a brisk breeze," she said. She
pulled her scarf from her sack. She
wrapped it around Hattie's neck.
"There. Better?"

Nearby, an owl hooted loudly in
the trees. Startled, Hattie jumped.

"Sophie, where *are* we?"

Sophie looked down at her map. 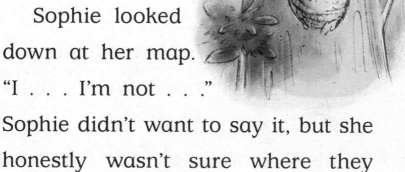 "I . . . I'm not . . ." Sophie didn't want to say it, but she honestly wasn't sure where they were.

Hattie's look of fear was back, and now Sophie was feeling it too. She checked her sack. They had only a few biscuits left and little bit of water. But worst of all, they were lost! And it was all Sophie's fault! What if they couldn't find their way home?

Sophie couldn't help thinking: Would they end up just like the squirrel in the story?

Just then, there was a rustling in the bushes right beside them. Sophie and Hattie grabbed each other's hands. Too afraid to run, they stood frozen to their spot.

Then they saw it—a bushy gray tail sticking up from behind some leafy branches!

Sophie and Hattie squeezed each other tighter. They kept their eyes glued on the tail as it moved toward them—closer and closer and closer.

chapter 7

The Way to Weedsnag Way

With a sudden crack of branches, something with gray fur landed right at Sophie's and Hattie's feet.

"Aaaaaahhh!" they cried. They covered their eyes in fear of the ferocious, monstrous . . .

"Squirrel?" said Sophie, peeking between her hands.

With a flick of his twitchy tail,

the squirrel tilted his head to one side, then smiled a big, friendly smile! "Afternoon! The name's Harry. Harry Higgins. Sorry if I scared you. I couldn't help overhearing. Do you need help finding your way?"

Sophie and Hattie looked at each

other in disbelief—and relief. "Why
yes!" Sophie replied. "We could use
a little advice."

"Well, well, well," said Harry,
"I'm happy to help. I've lost my way
before. No fun, no fun. Where are
you headed?"

Hattie spoke up. "Have you heard of a place called Weedsnag Way?"

"Where the emerald berries grow?" Sophie added.

Harry Higgins' eyes went wide with surprise. "Emerald berries? Weedsnag Way? *That's* where you're going?"

Sophie got ready for another warning—just like Zoe's.

But she was wrong. Instead, Harry Higgins wiggled his

whiskers and chuckled. "Of course I know how to get there. That's where I live!"

"It *is*?" cried Sophie.

"Are we close?" asked Hattie.

Harry nodded. "Follow me!"

Sophie couldn't believe their luck. She'd been about to give up—to tell Hattie they were lost. But they'd found the perfect guide!

They excitedly followed Harry. He led them down a slope, over a rock pile, through a curtain of weeping willows—and then he stopped.

"Here we are!" he said. "Welcome to Weedsnag Way."

Sophie peeked around him. For the second time that day, she gasped at the sight she saw. Hundreds of emerald-green bushes lined the path on both sides. Long branches arched over the path, making a tunnel. The sparkling berries—dozens on each

bush—made it look like a deep green sky filled with twinkling stars.

Sophie, Hattie, and Harry walked slowly through the arcade. Sophie reached out and picked one of the berries. She squished it between her fingers. The berry juice was a gorgeous shimmering green with blue flecks.

"Perfect!" Sophie cried. "What an amazing paint color this will make!" She explained to Harry how she'd seen a dress dyed with emerald berry juice. "That's why I was so eager to find some."

Harry nodded. "Oh, I understand," he said. "Do you know . . . *I* was drawn here by the emerald berries too. I used to make and sell hats. One day I saw a swan wearing a beautiful hat pin made with emerald berries. I wanted to make one just

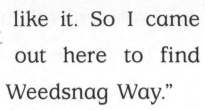

like it. So I came out here to find Weedsnag Way."

Harry paused, then added, "Unfortunately, I got a little lost. I found Weedsnag Way. Then I realized I didn't know the way home! Can you believe it?" Harry laughed. "It turned out okay, though. I decided I liked it here very much and wanted to stay." He sighed a small sigh. "But now and then I *do* miss Pine Needle Grove."

Hattie's jaw dropped. Sophie's

eyes went wide. Sophie and Hattie looked at each other.

Harry Higgins was the squirrel from the story—the squirrel who never returned from Weedsnag Way!

— chapter 8 —

Harry Higgins's Home

"Harry!" Sophie exclaimed. *"We're from Pine Needle Grove too!"*

Harry chittered in surprise. "You are?" he cried. "Well, what a day, what a day! Visitors from Pine Needle Grove!" He scurried off down Weedsnag Way. Then he stopped. He turned and waved for Sophie and Hattie to follow. "This calls for tea!

Come, I'll show you my house."

Sophie and Hattie followed Harry halfway down Weedsnag Way. There, a tall tree grew out from the middle of the berry bushes.

Sophie and Hattie watched as Harry scrambled up the tree trunk. When he got up to a large branch, he turned and looked down. "Stand back!" he called.

The girls stepped back as Harry dropped something down. It unrolled

down the length of the
trunk. The end of it came
to rest at the base of the
tree.

"A rope ladder!" Sophie
said in surprise.

"I've been waiting to use
this! Come on up!" Harry
called.

Hattie climbed carefully
up. Sophie followed right
behind her.

"Welcome," said Harry,
standing at the door of his
little squirrel house. It was

built right where the branch and the tree trunk met.

Harry led them inside a comfortable one-room home. Sophie looked around at the tiny wood stove, the handmade table and stools, and the

pine-wood bed with its pine-needle mattress.

"Please, sit!" said Harry. "Make yourself at home while I get the tea going."

But Sophie was too excited to

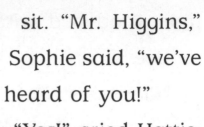

sit. "Mr. Higgins," Sophie said, "we've heard of you!"

"Yes!" cried Hattie. "You're famous in Pine Needle Grove!"

Harry wrinkled his nose. "Famous? Me?" he said. "But . . . what do you mean?"

Together, Sophie and Hattie explained. They told Harry that when he hadn't returned, folks back home decided something very awful had happened to him.

"Everyone thinks Weedsnag Way

is dangerous and scary," said Sophie.

Harry shook his head. "Oh, no, no, no. You two can plainly see. It's not scary at all. It *is* darker, I suppose, because of all the tall trees."

"And colder," Hattie pointed out.

She pulled Sophie's scarf tighter around her neck. "It *is* colder."

Harry nodded. "Perhaps. But I think it's the most beautiful place in the world."

Harry made the tea. Then the three of them sat chatting and laughing.

They imagined what the animals of
Pine Needle Grove would say if they
could see them at that very moment.

Outside Harry's round window, Hattie noticed the shadows getting longer. "Sophie, I think we'd better start for home."

"You're right," Sophie replied. Then she felt a pang of panic as

something dawned on her.

She didn't know the way home!

Oh, what do I say to Hattie? How can I tell her we're lost—just like Harry?

As if reading her mind, Hattie looked right at Sophie and said, "Don't worry. I know how to get home."

chapter 9

Hattie's Secret

Sophie couldn't believe her ears. "What? You know the way home?"

Hattie nodded confidently.

"But . . . but how?" Sophie asked. Then something occurred to her. "Hattie, did *you* know that *I* didn't know where we were?"

Hattie shrugged. "Not exactly," she said. "But back at the waterfall,

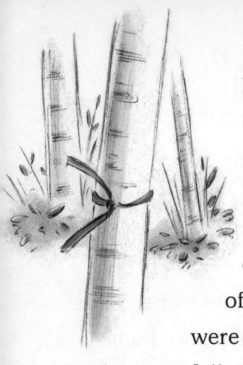

you didn't seem so sure. So just in case, I thought I'd leave a trail." Hattie pulled a handful of long reeds out of her pocket. They were just like the ones at the waterfall. "I tied reeds around some of the thinner tree trunks along the way."

Sophie gasped. So *that's* what Hattie had been doing! She hadn't been studying the trees, after all.

"Hattie, you're a genius!" Sophie

cried. "Now we just need to follow the trail back the way we came."

Hattie nodded. Sophie threw her arms around her and hugged her tight. "Oh, Hattie!" she cried. "Thank you! Thank you for being so careful and practical!"

Hattie's green face blushed pink. "You're welcome," she said with a laugh. Then she turned to Harry. "Mr. Higgins, would you like to come with us? We can take you back to Pine Needle Grove."

Harry thought it over. Then he said, "No, thank you! I don't have any family there. And really, Weedsnag Way is my new home. But you're welcome to come visit me again any time."

Sophie and Hattie smiled. "We will!"

"And when you do," Harry added, "might you bring me something from that wonderful little bakery in town? Perhaps a marigold cupcake with blueberry icing?" Harry rubbed his tummy.

Sophie laughed. "We could do that!" she said. "In fact, I know the owner very well."

chapter 10

The Whole Truth

Passing back through Weedsnag Way, Sophie gathered enough of the emerald berries to fill her pockets *and* Hattie's. Then Harry led them back to the spot where they'd met. The girls said good-bye to their new friend and set off for home.

They had no trouble following Hattie's trail back to the waterfall.

From there, they then followed the river upstream. They crossed the fallen log to the other side. The map showed them the rest of the way home.

Sophie dropped Hattie off at her house. "Do you think anyone will believe what we found in Weedsnag Way?" Sophie asked.

Hattie smiled. "Either way, we know the truth."

Sophie reached her house just

before dark. Inside, she dropped her sack by the front door. Her dad was in the kitchen, cooking dinner— carrot stew by the smell of it. Her mother and brother were on the sofa playing cards. Sophie smiled. She was so happy to be home.

"Well, hello, stranger!" George Mouse called from the kitchen. "That must have been quite a hike. You've been gone all day!"

Sophie hesitated. She knew she had to tell her family about her adventure. Over dinner, she told them the whole story. Her mom and dad listened without saying a word. But Sophie could tell by their

faces, they were not pleased.

"I know," Sophie said. "I should have told you. The map was not right, and we could have gotten lost. I was lucky to have Hattie with me."

Mr. and Mrs. Mouse looked at each other. Sophie got ready for a scolding.

"Please do not ever venture so far off again without telling us," her mother said to her sternly.

"I won't," said Sophie. "I promise."

Mr. Mouse cleared his throat. "And another thing!" he said.

Uh-oh, thought Sophie. *Here it comes.*

But her dad smiled and held out his hand. "Let's have a look at these emerald berries!"

That evening, Sophie tried out her brand-new paint color, emerald berry. She painted a beautiful scene of Weedsnag Way, with a waterfall way off in the distance.

Rising up from the emerald berry bushes was a tree with a rope ladder hanging down the trunk.

And there, at the top of the long ladder, stood one happy squirrel.

The End

the adventures of
SOPHIE MOUSE

Forget-Me-Not Lake

Contents

chapter 1

Mouse Life

Sophie Mouse skipped around the toadstool table. She added a carved-twig spoon to each of the four place settings.

"Napkin on the *left*, Winston," she told her little brother as they set the table for dinner. "Spoon on the right."

"Okay, Sophie," replied Winston. "Wait. Which side is left again?"

Sophie tried to be patient as she reminded him. She took a deep breath. Her nose twitched. Her whiskers quivered with glee. Delicious aromas filled the Mouse family's house in the hollow of a big oak tree.

Sophie's father, George Mouse, was at the stove. He was stirring a big pot of radish soup.

Sophie's mother, Lily Mouse, peeked into the oven. She was trying out a new recipe—clover and juniper berry cake.

Sophie came over to look at the

cake too. "We should *probably* try it before you add it to the bakery menu." She smiled sweetly at her mother. "Don't you think?"

Lily Mouse owned the only bakery in Pine Needle Grove. She was

known for making the most delicious cakes and pastries—often with
unexpected ingredients.

Lily Mouse smiled back at Sophie.
"Yes, of course," she said. "We will
all have a test piece—*after* dinner!"

Before long, the soup was ready.
George Mouse ladled it into walnut-
shell bowls. Then all four mice sat
down for Friday night dinner.

As they slurped their soup, Sophie and Winston had lots to tell about their week at school. Mrs. Wise, their teacher at Silverlake Elementary, had assigned the students a fun project.

"We have to prepare a presentation about our own species," Sophie

explained. "The frog students will talk about frogs. The birds will talk about birds. And the mice will talk about mice. Next week, we'll each give our presentations to the class. It's to help us learn more about one another."

Winston's eyes were wide with excitement. "And since we're both mice, Sophie and I get to work together!" he added.

Winston was six years old. It was the first year he was old enough to come to school at the schoolhouse.

"Winston suggested we say that mice are fast and can scurry places quickly," Sophie pointed out.

"And Sophie said we should talk about how we're small and can fit into tiny spaces," Winston added.

George Mouse smiled. "Very true," he said. "Can you think of other things we mice are good at?"

Sophie and Winston thought it over. Winston put his elbow on the table and rested his chin in his hand. Sophie gazed out the window, puzzling over the question.

But neither one could think of anything. Something was distracting them. They both sniffed the air.

Their whiskers twitched.

They looked at each other. Then they shouted it out together.

"The cake is ready!"

chapter 2

A Sunny Saturday

Sophie sat up in bed. She yawned and stretched. Sun streamed in through the knothole window.

"A perfect day to play at the lake!" she cried. She and her friends Hattie and Owen had made plans. They were going to meet at Forget-Me-Not Lake after breakfast.

Sophie jumped out of bed and

hurried to get dressed. As she pulled on her jumper, she paused. Her latest painting sat just where she'd left it on her easel. It was of a beautiful marigold she had seen the other day.

"Maybe this evening I'll paint a scene of our day at the lake," Sophie said to herself. She couldn't wait to use her new color, cornflower blue. She'd made it by grinding up bright-blue cornflower petals. "With a touch of green it could be just right for painting the water!"

Sophie ran downstairs. Winston and Mrs. Mouse were nibbling on freshly baked peach and poppy seed muffins.

Sophie reminded her mom that she was running off to meet Hattie and Owen.

"Okay," said Mrs. Mouse. "But have some breakfast first!"

Sophie grabbed a muffin. Then she took two more for Hattie and Owen. She wrapped them up in a linen napkin and tied it into a bundle.

"Your father is working today," Mrs. Mouse said. Mr. Mouse was the town architect. He was overseeing the construction of a rabbit's new house. "Winston will come with me to the bakery. Come find us there if you need anything.

And be home in time for dinner!"

"I will!" Sophie cried. She grabbed the napkin bundle and headed for the door. Then she stopped and turned. "And Winston, let's work on our project tonight!"

She heard Winston cheer as she headed out into the fresh air.

Forget-Me-Not Lake was a pretty long walk from Sophie's house. She headed toward town, then turned off onto the path that led to the lake. Along the way, she passed Oak Hollow Theater. Sophie had gone there once to see a play. The audience sat on carved-out logs that were arranged in rows on a slight

slope. The stage was at the bottom. In that log, there were several large holes. When the setting sun hit at just the right angle, it streamed through the holes and made spotlights that lit up the stage. Sophie thought it was beautiful.

Finally, the path came out of the woods. Sophie was standing on the bank of a big, glistening lake. It was surrounded by forget-me-nots—tiny blue flowers with yellow centers

that bloomed in bunches on little green stems. That's why it was called Forget-Me-Not Lake.

Very close by, a voice made Sophie jump. "Finally! We were wondering

when you'd get here!"
Sophie turned.
Her friend Owen
was hanging from
a tree. His tail was
wound around a low
branch.

"Owen! You startled
me!" Sophie cried. Then
she laughed. "You're too
good at sneaking up on me."

"Sorry," said Owen. "I
can't help it. That's just how
we snakes are, I guess."

His eyes lit up. "Hey! I should add that to my presentation for school!"

Sophie looked around. "Where's Hattie?" she asked.

Owen looked around too. "Huh," he said. "She was just here. Hattie! HAT-tie!"

There was no answer.

Sophie tried. "HAT-TIE! Where are you?" She turned to Owen. "Where could she have gone?"

— chapter 3 —

Green with
Frog Envy

SPLASH!

Suddenly, in a flash of green, Hattie broke the still surface of the water. She leaped out of the lake and landed right at Sophie's side. Water droplets flew off of her and onto Sophie.

"Whoa!" Sophie cried. "Good underwater hiding place!"

"Did I surprise you?" Hattie asked hopefully. Usually it was Sophie or Owen who won at hide-and-seek.

Sophie nodded and unwrapped her napkin bundle. "I brought treats from my mom," she said.

"Yum!" exclaimed Owen.

The three friends climbed onto a large rock that was sitting in the shallow water. They sat down and nibbled muffins while they talked.

They had just been together the day before at school. But they never ran out of things they *had* to tell one another.

"This morning, a groundhog popped up from under our kitchen floor!" Owen shared. "He said he must have taken a wrong turn. He promised to fix the hole. But you should have seen my mom's face!"

Hattie and Sophie giggled.

Then Hattie shared her exciting news. "My parents are going out tonight. And Lydie's going to watch me!" Lydie was Hattie's big sister. "She said she'd show me how to make braided ribbon-grass bracelets!"

Soon, the friends' talk turned to the school project. "I've started working on mine," Owen said. "But I can't think of many cool things that snakes can do."

Sophie and Hattie looked at Owen as if he were crazy. "What do you mean?" said Hattie. "You can reach way up high and way down low with your tail, for one thing."

"Yeah!" Sophie agreed. "Remember how you saved me? That time I fell into that hole in the meadow? You lowered your tail all the way down so I could climb out!"

Owen smiled proudly. "That's true," he said, remembering. "Oh! And I just thought of something else!"

Owen dove into the water—*splash!*—and stayed under.

"What is he doing?" Sophie asked.

"I have no idea. Oh, wait!" cried

Hattie, pointing. "Look at all those patterns on the surface! Owen is making them!"

Sophie watched the *S*-shaped wavelets ripple across the water, catching glints of sunlight. It was so beautiful!

Owen came up at last, and Sophie and Hattie clapped.

"I wish *I* could do that!" said Hattie wistfully. "Being a frog isn't all that fun, I guess."

Sophie gasped. "What?!" she said.

"But Hattie," Owen said, "you can hop farther than anyone!"

Hattie seemed to think about it for a minute. Then she got a twinkle in her eye. She hopped off the rock onto a lily pad. She bounced to another, and another. Finally, she hopped into the air, flipped, and did a swan dive into the water.

When she came up from underwater, Sophie and Owen cheered.

"Amazing!" Sophie called.

"Wow!" Owen cried.

Sophie felt it was her turn now.
"Winston and I have started making a list of things mice can do," she

said. Which cool thing should she demonstrate for her friends? Sophie ran through the list in her mind.

But as she did, Sophie's heart sank. Scurrying quickly and fitting into small spaces didn't seem so

interesting. Sophie kind of wished *she* could make cool water patterns or do perfect dives into the lake. But Sophie had never learned how to swim.

For the first time since Mrs. Wise gave the assignment, Sophie felt a

pang of doubt. She didn't say it out loud. She knew her friends would say she was being silly. But Sophie wondered. . . .

Was being a *mouse* the least exciting of all?

odd one out

Just then, a flock of ducks flew by. Sophie, Hattie, and Owen were distracted, watching them splash down on the far side of the lake.

Lucky ducks, thought Sophie. *They can swim* and *fly!*

"So," said Hattie, "what should we do today?"

Sophie tried to push her doubts

out of her mind. After all, it was a sunny Saturday in Silverlake Forest. The friends had nothing to do all day except have fun.

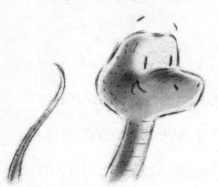

"Ooh!" said Owen excitedly. "We could swim across the lake. We could race!"

"Or we could judge each other's diving!" Hattie suggested.

Sophie didn't say anything. She didn't want to spoil their fun. But she couldn't do either one of those things.

It didn't take long for Hattie to realize it too. "Wait. That's no fun," said Hattie. "Let's think of something all three of us can do together."

Sophie smiled. She loved how Hattie could almost always tell what she was thinking.

"How about tag?" said Owen.

Sophie shrugged. Hattie did too. They played tag a lot at school during recess.

"Lily pad hopping?" Sophie said. She and Hattie did that a bunch when it was just the two of them at the lake. Sophie rode on Hattie's

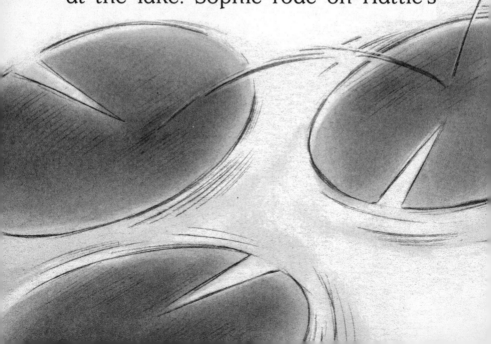

back while she jumped from one lily pad to another.

But Hattie couldn't carry Owen and Sophie at the same time. Plus Sophie could tell it wasn't what her friends *really* wanted to do.

"You know what?" said Sophie at last. "You two play in the water. I'll go pick some flowers to use for paint."

Hattie squinted at Sophie. "I don't know," she said uncertainly.

"Are you sure?" Owen asked.

Sophie nodded. "Yes, it's really okay!" she replied. And she meant it. It would be good to gather a bunch of paint supplies. She was running low at home.

Plus, thought Sophie, *when Hattie and Owen are done in the water, we'll do something else—all together.*

So Sophie wandered along the shore of the lake. She picked buttercups to use to make buttercup yellow paint. She found pink clover flowers to make clover pink.

She glanced over at the lake. Hattie and Owen were splashing each other.

Sophie wandered some more. She picked some tiny wild strawberries for making berry, berry red.

Hattie's voice and Owen's laugh drifted over on the breeze. Sophie looked their way to see them lining up to race across the lake.

Soon Sophie had ingredients for making at least ten different colors. She sat down on the shore of the lake and watched Hattie and Owen play. They were bobbing up for air. Then they were returning underwater to speak in bubble-talk.

The minutes dragged by. Sophie tried hard not to feel left out. After

all, she had told them to go ahead and play in the water. She just didn't think they'd do it for *so long*.

Sophie sighed. *Here we are at Forget-Me-Not Lake,* she thought. *So why does it feel like my friends have forgotten me?*

chapter 5

Library Quest

The rest of Sophie's day with her friends was much better. They skipped rocks on the water. They found ripe blackberries to snack on. They played leap frog along the path back to town.

Even so, when Sophie got home, she didn't feel like working on the school project. "We'll do it tomorrow," she told Winston, who met her at the front door.

The next morning, Sophie woke up in a better mood. It helped that what woke her was the scent of her mother's rosemary-mint scones wafting upstairs.

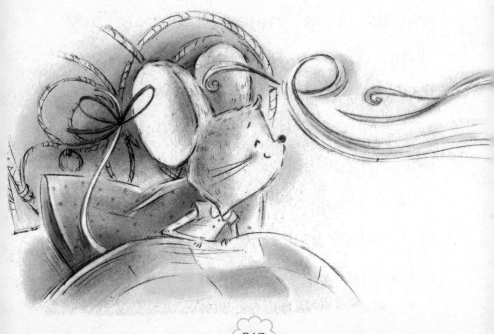

She also woke up with an idea. She and Winston could go to the library later. Maybe they'd find books with some *really* fascinating facts about mice!

First the siblings had to do their morning chores. Sophie swept out the bedrooms and hung the wet laundry to dry. Winston gathered dandelion greens for that night's salad and

counted how many vegetables were left in the root cellar. Lily Mouse said it was good counting practice.

When they were finished, they walked into town with their mother. She headed for the bakery while Sophie and Winston went off to the library. "Come have a snack when you're done!" she called after them.

The library was the oldest and biggest building in town. Inside,

wooden shelves of books rose up to the ceiling. Tall ladders on wheels helped the librarians reach the top shelves.

Sophie and Winston went right to the young readers' section in the back. They saw two of their friends sitting at a tree-stump table: their rabbit classmates, Ben and his little brother, James.

Sophie said hello and Winston hurried to James's side. The two younger siblings were the same age. They usually sat next to each other at school.

"Are you here working on your project too?" Winston asked.

James nodded. He pointed to a picture in the book he was reading.

"Did you know that we rabbits can swivel our eyes *all the way around*?!" James asked.

"So we can see behind us without turning our heads, Ben added.

Winston's jaw dropped. "That is so cool!" he cried in awe.

Sophie smiled politely. *Another thing mice can't do,* she thought to herself.

Sophie wandered off to find the books on mice. At the end of a row of shelves, she found Malcolm Mole reading in a comfy corner.

"Hey, Sophie!" he said. "Did you know moles can dig up to eighteen feet in one hour?"

Sophie shook her head. "I did not know that," she said. She knew for

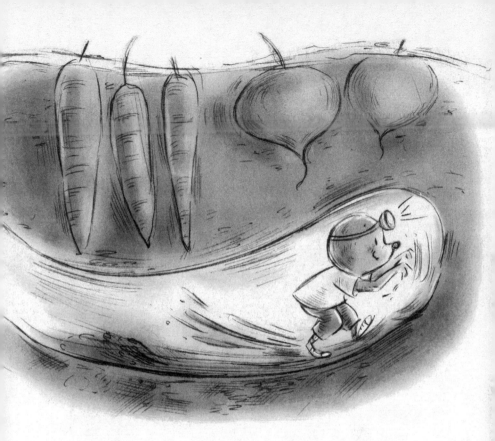

sure that mice couldn't do that either.

In front of the section of animal books, Sophie found Piper, her hummingbird friend. She was hovering in front of the hummingbird books.

"Sophie, isn't this just the best project?" Piper said. "I didn't know that we're the only birds that can fly backward!"

Sophie gulped. It seemed like everyone in class had something exciting to share in their presentation. She scanned the shelves for mouse books. With a sigh of relief, she found them. They were right between the books on mountain lions and musk oxen.

Then Sophie had a terrible thought: What if they didn't have any amazing mouse facts in them after all?

— chapter 6 —

The Swim Lesson

Sophie found five books about mice. She carried the stack to an empty table. Then she sat down and started flipping through them.

She read about what mice liked to eat.

Sophie shrugged. "Boring," she said.

She read about mice and climbing.

Everyone knows that, she thought. Then she turned the page.

Sophie's heart was racing with excitement—and nervousness. She had never met a swimming mouse before! She bet most of her class-mates hadn't either.

What if she, Sophie Mouse, could learn to swim? *That* would be an exciting tidbit for the presentation! This book made it sound like something she *could* do—if she had the courage to try.

"Okay!" said Hattie. "Let's review our water safety rules!"

Sophie, Hattie, and Owen were back at Forget-Me-Not Lake. Sophie

had asked her friends to give her a swim lesson. But now . . . Sophie was having second thoughts.

"First, we'll all stay in the shallow

water," Hattie was saying. "Second, we must stick together. Third, either Owen or I will have our eyes on Sophie whenever she is trying to swim."

"Agreed!" said Owen.

Sophie took a deep breath. *I can do this,* she told herself, and tried to believe it.

With her friends on either side of her, Sophie slowly waded

into the lake. It was cool on her legs as she went deeper and deeper.

When Sophie was waist deep, Hattie stopped. "This is good," she said. "Let's get you used to this depth."

Sophie smiled uncertainly. The water felt really . . . *wet*. A shiver went up her spine.

"Now let's try floating." Hattie suggested.

Hattie demonstrated. She lay back on the surface of the water. She stretched her arms and legs out to the sides and—*ta-da*!

Owen was also floating on the

surface. "The water holds us up," said Owen.

Doubt crept into Sophie's mind. "Hmm. That looks tricky," she said.

Hattie stood up. "Don't worry," she said. "We'll help you."

Sophie's friends stood close on

either side of her. They held on to her as she started to lie back into the water. "Good," said Hattie. "We've got you. Tilt your head waaaaay back."

Sophie got about halfway there. But she just couldn't lie all the way back. It didn't feel natural. Plus, she was worried about getting water in her ears!

Sophie jumped up suddenly. "Um, I'm not sure I can do that . . . yet," she said.

"That's okay!" said Hattie. "We'll try something else."

They showed Sophie how they could dunk their heads underwater

and try to sit on the bottom of the
lake. "Take a deep breath," said
Owen.

"And hold it!" added Hattie.

"And just sit down in the water!"
finished Owen.

Hattie and Owen did it. They made it look so easy!

Sophie's friends popped up. Now it was her turn. She took a deep breath and held it. She got ready to go under and . . .

She couldn't do it.

"How about just getting wet up to your neck?" Owen said.

Sophie nodded. "One . . . two . . . three . . . ," she counted.

Then she froze. Her knees wouldn't bend.

Sophie's shoulders drooped. "Oh," she groaned, feeling frustrated. "This isn't going to work. Thanks for trying, you guys." She turned and leaped out of the lake.

"Sophie, wait!" Hattie called after her.

"Come back!" cried Owen.

But Sophie hit dry land and ran all the way home.

— chapter 7 —

A Sophie-Size Surprise

At home Sophie's dad was reading a book in the living room. She changed out of her swimsuit and flopped onto her bed.

By then, Sophie was all out of tears. When George Mouse knocked to see if she was okay, she said she was fine.

"I'm just painting," Sophie called

to him. But really, she lay there, staring at the ceiling. She was painting a picture in her *mind*.

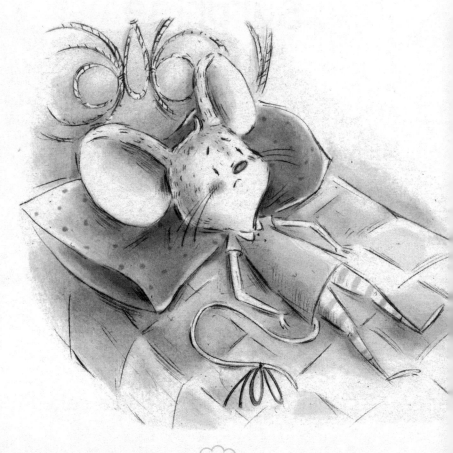

It was a sunny-day scene of Forget-Me-Not Lake. A frog and a snake were racing each other across the lake.

On the shore, one little mouse was waiting for them.

Sophie looked over at her easel. A
blank canvas sat there, waiting. She
had the painting all worked out. But
she didn't actually want to paint it.

She realized she hated the idea of
going underwater. Even if mice *could*
learn to swim, Sophie didn't want

to. Not anytime soon. She wasn't going to be the Incredible Swimming Mouse, after all. And she still didn't have any exciting mouse facts to include in the presentation.

Sophie moped in her room. At one point she heard her mom's and

Winston's voices down-
stairs. She figured they
were home from the
bakery.

A little while
later there was
another knock at
Sophie's bedroom
door. "Come in,"
Sophie called.

The door opened
and Hattie and Owen
stuck their heads in.
Sophie sat up straight.
"Oh!" she said, surprised.

"W-what are you two doing here?"

Owen wiggled forward. "We're sorry the swim lesson didn't go so well," he said.

Sophie shrugged. "That's okay," she said gloomily. "Guess I'm just not a swimmer."

Hattie sat down on the end of Sophie's bed. "We want to make it up to you," she said. Then she smiled slyly. "In fact, we have a little surprise for you!"

Sophie couldn't help being curious. "A surprise?" she said. "What *kind* of surprise?"

Hattie and Owen wouldn't tell her.

Instead, Hattie took Sophie's hand.

"Just come with us."

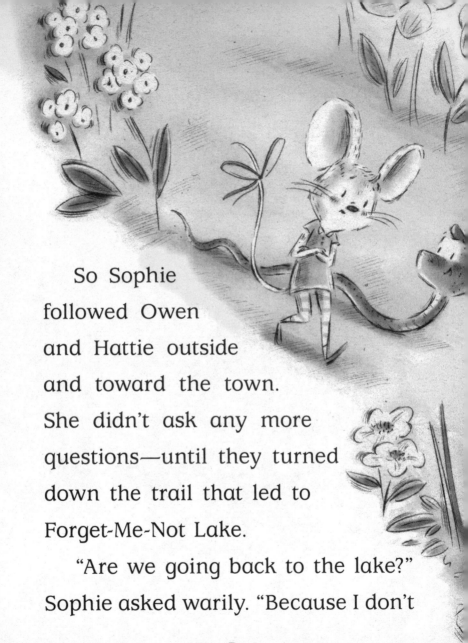

So Sophie
followed Owen
and Hattie outside
and toward the town.
She didn't ask any more
questions—until they turned
down the trail that led to
Forget-Me-Not Lake.

"Are we going back to the lake?"
Sophie asked warily. "Because I don't

really want more lessons."

Her friends led her on. "Just come on," said Owen.

They walked farther. They were nearly at the lake.

Sophie added, "Mice might be able to swim. But I'll never be the kind of swimmer you two are. You'll have more fun without me."

"Sophie," said Hattie, "wait until you see the surprise!"

They walked a little more. Soon they were standing in some tall reeds on the lake shore. Hattie and Owen parted the curtain of reeds at the water's edge.

Floating in the lake was a raft. It was made of twigs tied together with long blades of grass. Resting on top of the raft was a twig paddle.

Sophie noticed it was just the right size for a mouse.

Smells Like Trouble

Right away, Sophie realized what her friends had done—and why.

Owen smiled. "Just because you're not a swimmer—yet—doesn't mean we can't all have fun together in the water."

"Or *on* the water," said Hattie. She gave Sophie a nudge toward the raft. "Go ahead! Try it out!"

Sophie took a hesitant step toward the raft.

"Oh, wait!" Hattie said. "I made this for you—just to be extra safe." Hattie placed a vest made of seed-pods over Sophie's head. There was a dangling string that Hattie tied around Sophie's waist. "It floats!"

Hattie explained. "And it would keep you afloat, too—if needed."

Sophie smiled and carefully stepped onto the raft. She sat down and picked up the paddle. Hattie and Owen gave the raft a gentle push and she was off!

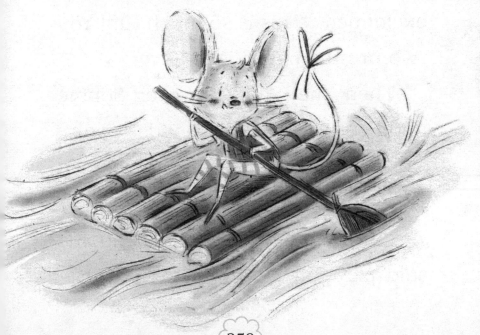

Sophie beamed as she paddled around. Hattie and Owen jumped into the water. They swam around her raft. They splashed water at Sophie. She splashed them back using her paddle.

"Oh, thank you both!" Sophie exclaimed. "This is so much fun! You two are the best friends ever."

Then they had a race. Sophie paddled while her friends swam. Hattie won, but Sophie came in a close second.

"Next time, look out!" Sophie said playfully. "With more practice,

I might get even faster!"

The three friends lost all track of time. They played at the lake for most of the afternoon.

Suddenly, in the middle of a game of water tag, Sophie froze. Her nose and whiskers twitched. She tilted her head back and sniffed the air.

"Do you smell that?" she asked Hattie and Owen.

They sniffed the air too. "Smell what?" asked Owen.

"I don't smell anything," said Hattie.

Sophie sniffed again, just to be sure. "Yep. It's about to rain—a lot."

Hattie's brow wrinkled with worry. "We'd better get home then!" she said uneasily.

The friends tied up the raft along the shore. Then, together, they hurried for home.

"It's a good thing you told us!" Owen said to Sophie as they went. "We could have gotten caught in the rainstorm!"

Sophie stopped in her tracks. "Owen!" she cried. "That's it! A mouse's sense of smell is . . . extraordinary! And it's good for more than just know-ing when cakes are ready!"

Hattie and Owen looked confused. But Sophie just smiled proudly as they hurried along. She couldn't wait to tell Winston that she had a great idea for their presentation!

Fun Facts

On Tuesday at school, all the students arrived ready to share their projects with the class. Mrs. Wise called each species up, one at a time, to do their presentation.

Sophie was curious to see what everyone else had done—and surprised to learn many things she did not know about them.

Of course she knew that most birds could fly. "But did you know that bird bones are hollow inside?" Zoe the bluebird said.

Sophie also learned that rabbits' teeth never stop growing. She learned that frogs can breathe through their skin. And she learned that squirrels

sometimes forget where they bur-
ied their acorns. "Forgotten acorns
can grow into oak
trees," said Ellie
the squirrel. "So
you could say
that squirrels
plant trees!"

Then it was
Sophie and
Winston's turn to
talk about mice. They
proudly showed off the
poster they'd made together. Sophie
had painted some pictures of mice

climbing, jumping, balancing, and squeezing through tight spaces. There was even one of a mouse swimming. "Mice *can* swim," Winston said. "But not all mice like to."

Sophie looked over at Hattie and Owen. They smiled at her.

Then Sophie pointed to the last picture—of a mouse sniffing the air. "Mice have a great sense of smell, and their whiskers can sense changes in temperature—which might be why I feel like I can 'smell' when the rain is coming!"

Sophie smiled. It was a really cool fact that she hadn't even known about herself before they'd done the project.

That night, in her bedroom, Sophie painted a beautiful scene of Forget-Me-Not Lake. In it, she was paddling across the lake on her raft, with Owen and Hattie swimming behind. They were racing, and Sophie was about to win.

Sophie stepped back to admire her work. Her new color, cornflower blue, was the perfect shade for the water.

The End

the adventures of
SOPHIE MOUSE
Looking for winston

Contents

— chapter 1 —

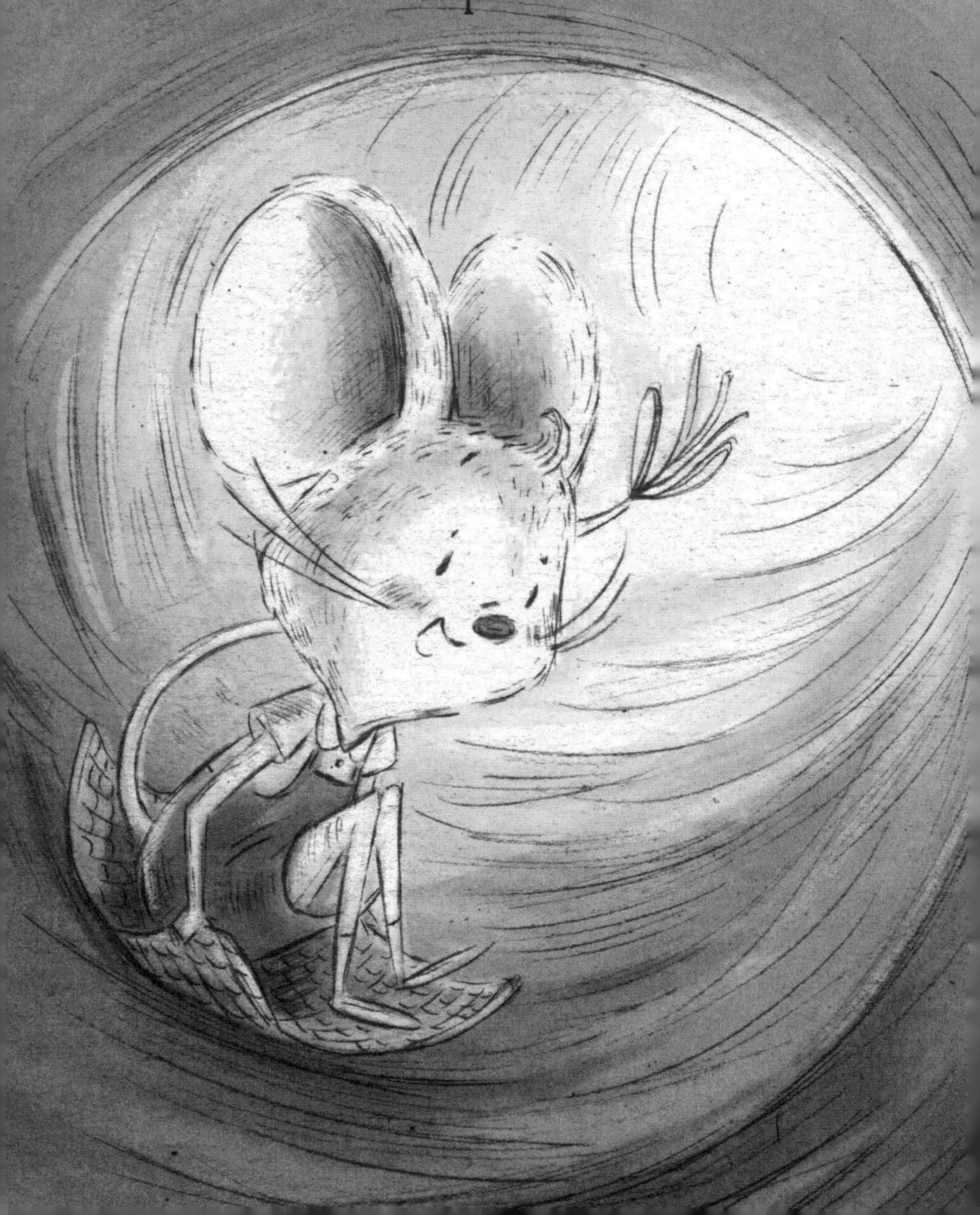

Fun with Friends

"Wheeeeeeeeeeee!" Sophie squealed with delight. Her voice echoed off the curved wooden walls of the giant tunnel slide. Sophie slid through the darkness. The slide twisted to the right. Then it turned to the left. Sophie grasped the fern she was sitting on. The slide track spiraled around and down, down, down, until—

Sophie came shooting out of the bottom end. *Fwomp!* She landed in a soft pile of green leaves.

High above, on a birch branch, Sophie's best friends cheered.

"Whoo-hoo!" cried Hattie Frog.

"Wow!" Owen Snake called out. "That's a long way down!"

Birch Tree Slide was a hollow, twisted branch. It leaned up against the trunk of a

huge birch tree. To get to the top of the slide, Sophie, Hattie, and Owen had first climbed way up the tree using its knotholes. Sophie had been excited to go first.

Hattie came down next. She disappeared into the tunnel. Sophie could hear her whooping all the way down. At the bottom, Hattie landed

next to Sophie in the leaves. They both laughed.

Sophie and Hattie had found Birch Tree Slide together when they were six years old. It felt like their secret place. Sophie had shown it to her brother, Winston. Hattie had shown it to her big sister, Lydie.

Now they had brought Owen. He

and his family had moved to Pine Needle Grove a while ago. But there were still lots of fun places Owen had never been.

"Come on, Owen!" Sophie called up. "Your turn!"

Owen didn't look so sure. He stayed coiled up, not moving. He seemed to be measuring the slide in his head.

"It's so much fun!" Hattie shouted. "We promise!"

Finally, Owen disappeared into the slide. Sophie could hear an "Aaaaaaaaah!" that sounded far away but grew louder and louder.

And then—*whoosh!*—there was Owen, jetting out of the bottom of the slide. His face looked panicked as he flew through the air. But when he hit the leaf pile—

Owen burst out laughing. "That is so fun!"

"Isn't it?!" Hattie cried.

Sophie patted Owen on the back. "Told you we'd have fun this weekend. Didn't we, Owen?"

The three friends had decided on

a project for the weekend: to take Owen to as many new places as possible.

Just then, a blue butterfly fluttered out of the trees. It circled Owen's head once, then flew on.

"Wow, what kind of butterfly was that?" Owen asked.

Hattie's brow wrinkled. "Probably a blue morpho."

"That reminds me," Sophie said with a gasp, "Owen hasn't been to Butterfly Brook!"

Hattie jumped up. "Oh yes!" she cried. "We have to take you there. It's the prettiest spot. And lots of different kinds of butterflies live there!"

"Sometimes," Sophie said, "if you are very still, they will land in your hand." Sophie glanced at Owen and quickly added, "Or on your head!"

Owen laughed. "I want to see it! Why don't we go tomorrow? Right after breakfast?"

Sophie frowned. She had chores to do after breakfast. "You two go on together in the morning. I'll do my chores fast and meet you there."

chapter 2

Sophie's Dream House

"Sorry I'm late!" Mrs. Mouse called. She had just stepped through the front door. "The bakery was so busy today!"

Sophie, Winston, and their dad were already sitting down at the table for dinner. Mr. Mouse had made spaghetti squash and a kale salad.

"I have something to add," said

Mrs. Mouse. She pulled a loaf of cranberry-nut bread from her bag. "Just out of the oven!"

Sophie's nose twitched and she smiled. She loved having a mom who owned a bakery!

"So what did I miss?" Mrs. Mouse asked.

Mr. Mouse served her salad. "I was just telling Sophie and Winston all about my new project," he said.

"I'm going to design a house for a turtle family."

"Guess what the best part is, Mom!" Sophie said.

But Winston couldn't wait for her to guess. He blurted out the answer. "They want it to look like a turtle shell on the outside!"

"Winston!" Sophie scolded. "I said for her to guess."

"Sorry," Winston mumbled. "I couldn't help it."

Mr. Mouse was an architect. He designed homes for animal families all over Silverlake Forest. Sophie loved to watch him do sketches at his drafting table. She thought she might like to design a house someday. Or maybe it would be even more fun to design a *play* house—or a fort! What would it be like, Sophie wondered. A little cottage with comfy chairs and reading nooks? A tree house with

ladders to go up and slides to come down? Or maybe a breezy, floating boat-fort on a babbling brook? Which reminded her . . .

"Hattie and I are taking Owen to Butterfly Brook tomorrow," Sophie

shared. "And I just decided: I think we should build a fort there!"

It would be the perfect spot—a fort in the woods that no one would know about. Well, except for Sophie's parents and Winston.

After dinner, Sophie sat on the couch reading a book. Winston sat next to her, tying knots in a long reed. He'd been doing that a lot lately.

Winston was trying to earn his knot-tying badge in Junior Forest Scouts.

"Sophie," said Winston, "can I come with you tomorrow to help build the fort?" He smiled up at her sweetly.

Sophie frowned. She didn't want to hurt Winston's feelings. But he *was* only six. She worried that he would get in the way.

"Sorry, Winston," Sophie said gently. "But you're too little. Building a fort is hard work." Seeing Winston's

smile disappear, she added, "How about this? I'll bring you to *see* the fort when we're all done. Okay?"

Winston looked down and nodded. He went on tying knot after knot without saying another word.

chapter 3

Footsteps in the Forest

Leaves crunched under Sophie's feet. It was still early in the morning. But Sophie's chores were done and she was already halfway to Butterfly Brook.

She shifted her satchel to her other shoulder. Inside she had water and snacks and her painting supplies— some brushes and berries. Sophie always brought art supplies with her in case she saw something she just *had* to paint. She was already thinking about the scene she'd paint after they finished their fort today.

Step by step, Sophie's feet carried her closer to Butterfly Brook. She

thought about the advice her dad
had given her about building.

"Try to use your strongest mate-
rials at the bottom of the structure,"
Mr. Mouse had said the night before.
"And don't forget about windows!
Light is important."

Sophie pictured a fort with a skylight— a big window in the ceiling. *Could we make something like that? Or maybe a fort with hanging vines for walls, so you could walk right*

through them! Or an underground fort with tunnels. Or—

"Ouch!" cried a little voice.

Sophie stopped in her tracks. Who had said that?

She looked all around and up into the trees. But Sophie didn't see any-one. All she heard now was a cricket chirping.

She shrugged and kept walking.

Crunch, crunch, crunch went the leaves under her feet. She walked and walked. Then, between two of her steps, she thought she heard other footsteps behind her.

Sophie stopped. The other footsteps stopped too. She turned.

There was no one there.

Sophie's fur pricked up on her

back. There was no reason to fear other animals in Silverlake Forest. But Sophie did feel like someone was following her. Why would they be hiding?

She walked on, faster this time. Faster and faster still. Then, suddenly, she whipped around.

This time, she saw something.

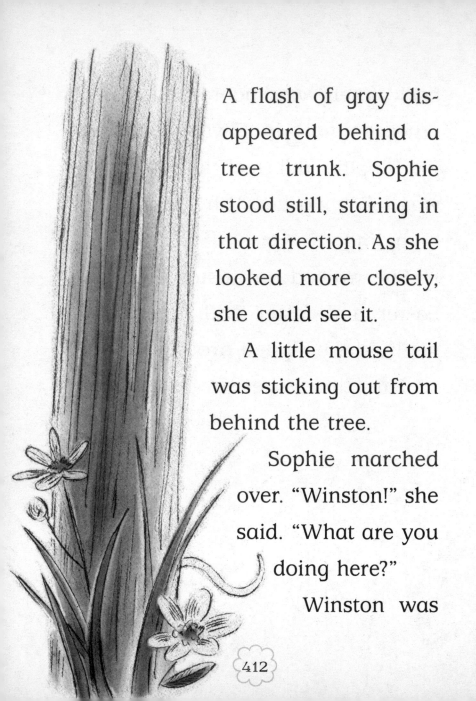

A flash of gray disappeared behind a tree trunk. Sophie stood still, staring in that direction. As she looked more closely, she could see it.

A little mouse tail was sticking out from behind the tree.

Sophie marched over. "Winston!" she said. "What are you doing here?"

Winston was

crouched down behind the tree. He stood up and smiled sheepishly at Sophie.

"You followed me?" Sophie asked her brother.

Winston nodded. "I wanted to

come and help build the fort," he said. "Can I? Pleeeease?"

Sophie sighed. "Do Mom or Dad know where you are?" she asked. "You can't just run off without telling them."

Winston nodded again. "Right after you left, I told them I was going with you. I ran to catch up." He looked down at the ground. "But I knew if you saw me, you'd tell me to go home."

Just then, Sophie noticed a scrape on Winston's knee.

Winston saw Sophie looking. "I

tripped over a tree root," he explained.

Ah-hah! thought Sophie. That was the "ouch" she'd heard.

Sophie opened her bag. She took out her water canteen and a hand-kerchief. She wet the handkerchief and used it to gently clean Winston's scrape.

"Winston," she said, "I told you. You're too little to help us. You need to go home and take care of your knee." She handed the handkerchief to Winston. "Here. You can take this with you."

Winston started to argue. "But I—"

"No buts!" Sophie said, putting on her best big-sister voice. "I told you not to come along. But you did anyway and *now* look. You need to go home, Winston."

Winston's shoulders fell. He kicked at some leaves. "You never let me go

anywhere with you," Winston said
as he shuffled away.

Sophie put her hands on her hips.
"That's not true!" she called.

But Winston didn't answer.

chapter 4

Butterfly Magic

Sophie turned and stomped toward Butterfly Brook. Sometimes Winston was so frustrating!

How is he supposed to help us? He's already hurt. What if he got even more hurt? I'm just looking out for him.

Still, Sophie felt bad. She knew there *was* another reason she didn't want Winston to come.

We'd spend more time looking after Winston than we would building. That wouldn't make any sense at all!

She walked and walked, but Sophie couldn't shake it. She kept thinking of the sad look on Winston's face.

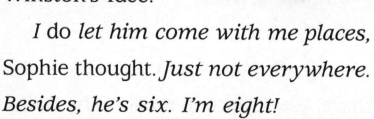

I do *let him come with me places,* Sophie thought. *Just not everywhere. Besides, he's six. I'm eight!*

At Butterfly Brook, Sophie met up with Hattie and Owen.

"You were right," said Owen, looking around. "This is amazing!"

Sophie's frustration with Winston faded as she looked around too. She had been here so many times. But it still felt magical to her. The

water in the narrow brook skipped
down the rocks. On either side of the
brook, evergreen trees grew in the
dappled sunshine. The trees' long
lower branches arched down toward

the ground. They created little hideaways underneath.

Sophie and Hattie led Owen to
one of the hideaways. They peeked
in. Dozens of butterflies fluttered in

the small space. There were bright
yellow ones, orange ones, and blue
ones, too.

"Blue morphos!" Owen whispered, pointing them out.

"Right!" whispered Hattie. "There are tons of different kinds of butter-flies here. They seem to like hiding out here under the branches."

The three friends watched the butterflies for a little while. Then they stepped out from under the branches.

Sophie rubbed her hands together. "So, I have an idea!" she said. "What do you say we build a fort—right here at Butterfly Brook?" Sophie told Hattie and Owen about the house her dad was designing for the turtle family. "It really got me . . . *inspired*!" Sophie said dreamily.

"I'm in!" said Owen.

Hattie nodded. "Let's do it!"

"All right!" said Sophie, clapping with excitement.

"I've been thinking about how we can build it."

Hattie laughed and gave Sophie a friendly squeeze. "Why am I not surprised?" she said.

chapter 5

The Design

They didn't waste any time. They scanned the area for building materials. They found lots of pine boughs on the ground.

"Maybe good for the roof!" Owen suggested.

They found plenty of rocks—large and small—on the bank of the brook.

"We could use these for the

foundation," said Hattie.

"Great!" said Sophie. "My dad did say to use the strongest materials at the bottom." Sophie stood and looked around. "But what we really need for the structure of the walls are a few sturdy sticks."

They searched and searched. Almost all the sticks and branches

on the ground
were the bendy
pine kind.

Finally
Owen called out,
"What about these?"

He had found two
long sticks under some leaves.

"I think they're perfect!" Sophie
said. "I wish there were more. But
maybe we could make a lean-to."

"A *what*-to?" Owen asked.

Sophie laughed. She walked over
to an evergreen tree. "My dad taught
me that a lean-to is usually a building

that is made when two things *lean* against something else. So we could lean our two sticks against this trunk," she said, patting the tree trunk.

"Oh! I get it," said Hattie. "The sticks would make our frame. And we can tie the pine boughs over the frame to make the walls!"

"Yes!" Sophie and Owen cried together.

They agreed on a plan. Hattie and Owen would gather as many pine boughs as they could. Meanwhile, Sophie would go find something they

could use to tie them together. She
knew where to find some reeds. She
walked downstream to gather them.

When Sophie got back, she had a
bundle of reeds.

"Let's see if this will work!" Sophie
said.

Hattie held a bunch of pine boughs
together. Sophie wrapped a reed
around them. But when she tried to
tie it, the knot slipped out.

Sophie tried again. Again, the knot slipped.

Hattie and Owen tried too. They tried double knots. They tried triple knots. But nothing worked.

"These reeds are too slippery," said Owen.

All of a sudden, Sophie thought of
someone: Winston! He was a Junior
Forest Scout. He had been learning
to make all kinds of knots. Sophie
bet he could tie a knot in the reed
that would *stay* tied.

Plus, Sophie knew how much Winston wanted to build with them. He would be so excited to help out!

Sophie told Hattie and Owen her idea. They agreed it was great, and Sophie scurried home to find Winston.

She ran the whole way, smil-
ing. She imagined what she'd say—
"Winston, we need you!"—and she
imagined the look on Winston's face.
Maybe he would even admit that
Sophie *did* let him do stuff with her.

Sophie was out of breath as she

ran into their house in the roots of the big oak tree. "Winston!" she called out. "WIN-ston!"

There was no answer. The house was silent. Sophie quickly checked upstairs. But she could tell right away, the house was empty.

Where was everyone? Where was Winston?

— chapter 6 —

Missing Mouse

Sophie spotted a note on the toad-stool table.

Dear Sophie,

When you and Winston get home, come find me at the library. I'll be working there this afternoon. Mom is at the bakery.

Love,
Dad

Sophie twirled her tail as she thought. Her dad must have left the note before Winston came back. Otherwise, it would say he *and Winston* were at the library.

So when Winston got home, no one was here, thought Sophie. She looked down at her dad's handwriting. *And Winston can't read cursive.*

Where would Winston have gone?

Probably to his favorite place, thought Sophie. The playground! It wasn't far. Their parents let him go there on his own. One day the week before, Winston had run off to play there before he'd even had breakfast. *Mom sure wasn't happy about that!* thought Sophie.

Sophie scurried down the path toward town. Before the first bend, she ducked down a side trail. It twisted through some maple trees. Then it came out into a big clearing—the playground.

Two of her rabbit friends from school were there. James, who was Winston's age, was on the rope swing. His big brother, Ben, was on the monkey bars. It was a small playground, but there was also a seesaw, a

climber, and a line of tree stumps
that Winston liked to hop across.

Sophie said hello. "Have you seen
Winston?" she asked.

Ben and James shook their heads.
"No," said James. "We've been here
all morning. He hasn't been here."

"Hmmmmm," Sophie said. "Okay. Thanks."

Sophie paused to think about where to check next. Maybe by the stream near Hattie's house? Tall reeds grew along the bank. Winston had been going there a lot to get reeds to practice tying knots.

Sophie scurried over to the stream. But Winston wasn't there, either.

Sophie tossed a pebble into the stream. The water rippled out from the splash. *Where else could Winston be?* she thought. *He wouldn't have gone to the bakery to find Mom. It's too far and he's not allowed to go alone. And he doesn't know Dad is at the library.*

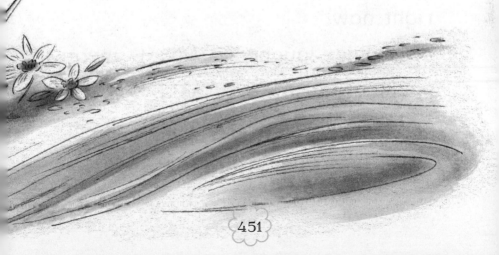

Suddenly Sophie noticed an older toad sitting on the bank downstream. She was reading the newspaper. Sophie hurried over to her.

"Excuse me," Sophie said politely. "Have you seen a little spotted mouse this morning?"

The toad looked up from her paper. She studied Sophie. "Seen one?" she said. "I'm looking at one right now!"

Sophie laughed. "No, I mean smaller than me," she said.

The toad put her paper down. "Well, now. I do recall seeing a mouse

earlier. I'm not sure, but I think he went that way." The toad pointed downstream.

Sophie gasped. "He did? Oh, thank you. Thank you so much!"

She skipped along downstream, happy to have a lead. She'd catch

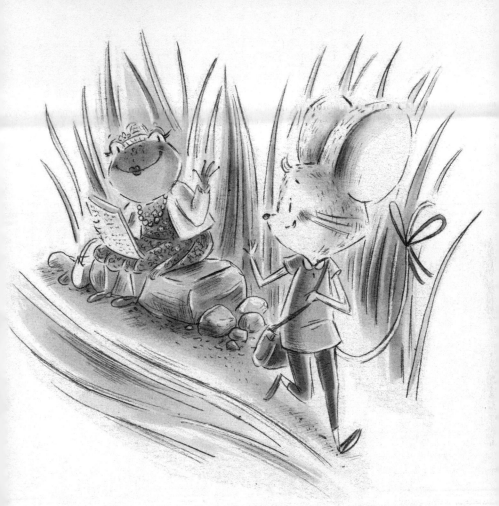

up with Winston. She'd give him the good news. And she'd get him to come back to Butterfly Brook.

— chapter 7 —

A Few Clues

At the next bend in the stream, Sophie had to slow down. The bank was muddy. She had to choose her path carefully. She looked down to plan her hops from rock to rock.

That's when she spotted them.

Fresh tracks in the mud!

Sophie stopped. She looked more closely. Yes! She was sure, now. They looked like mouse tracks!

Now I'm definitely on the right path! thought Sophie. *I will follow these mouse tracks wherever they lead. And at the end, I will find Winston!*

So Sophie followed the tracks. She followed them down the stream. They led to a spot where a log footbridge crossed the water.

Muddy mouse footprints led across the bridge. So Sophie crossed the bridge too.

On the other side, she found more tracks in the mud. And that wasn't all. Sophie spotted a little pile of nut shells between two of the footprints. Acorn shells! Winston's favorite!

The footprints and the trail of

acorn shells led upstream, so Sophie followed them along the stream bank. Finally, the tracks took a turn away from the water. They led out of the mud and into a thicket. On the firmer ground, Sophie couldn't see the tracks anymore.

But the trail of acorn shells led on. Sophie looked ahead into the dense underbrush. She saw a few more shells and made her way to them. Then she saw more farther on.

What was Winston doing coming this way? Sophie wondered. *It's not easy getting through here. And it's kind of far from home. Where was he going?*

Sophie kept following the trail of acorn shells. She ducked under

thorny vines. She climbed over fallen branches. She squeezed through a tight space between two rocks. And she parted a curtain of ivy.

Then she stopped. She was staring at a door—a wooden door in the side of a rocky mound. It was mouse-size. And it had a knocker.

Sophie did what any adventurous mouse would do: She knocked on the door.

Within seconds, it swung open. On the other side was an old gray mouse. He was wearing suspender trousers, a button-down shirt, and

a wool cap. He was nibbling on an acorn. Bits of shell fell onto the doorstep.

The mouse pulled a pair of glasses out of his shirt pocket. He put them on and peered through them at Sophie.

"What do you want?" he said, a bit grumpily.

For a moment Sophie was speechless. Then she blurted out, "You're not Winston!"

"Correct!" the old mouse said. "I'm not Winston!" And he shut the door firmly.

chapter 8

Walking in Circles

Sophie stood frozen to the spot. Her mouth hung open in surprise. She was too shocked to feel insulted.

She thought back to the toad reading the paper near Hattie's house. She said she'd seen a small gray mouse. And she had. It just wasn't Winston!

All this time, Sophie had been tracking the wrong mouse!

Sophie was worried. She realized she had no idea where Winston was. She was the one who had sent him home. And now he was missing. What if he was lost? Winston wasn't as good at finding his way around Silverlake Forest as she was.

Sophie looked up toward the sky. She sniffed the air. She saw moss growing on the north side of a tree trunk. She did some figuring in her head. She'd gone all the way from Butterfly

Brook, to her house, to the playground, to the stream. Then she had
tracked the mouse to where she was
now.

She realized she'd walked in one
big circle! That meant she was not
far from Butterfly Brook now.

Sophie made a decision. She had to tell her parents Winston was missing. Both of them were in town. The fastest way there would take her past Butterfly Brook. She'd stop on the way to tell Hattie and Owen what was going on.

Sophie set out at a quick pace. She really hoped her mom and dad knew what to do. As Sophie neared Butterfly Brook, she came to a mud puddle. A stick was standing straight up in the mud. Sophie hopped over the puddle and noticed some lines drawn in the mud. *That kind of looks like an* M, she thought as she hurried on.

Three steps later, Sophie stopped suddenly. She turned around and hurried back to the mud.

From this side, the *M* looked like . . . a *W*! A *W* for Winston!

Could Winston have drawn it? Could he actually be nearby?

"WIN-ston?" Sophie called out. "WINSTON!"

But there was no answer. All Sophie heard were birds chattering above and her own voice echoing off the tree trunks all around.

Sophie walked quickly on. She zipped through a tunnel of low-hanging branches. She darted around a briar patch. She sped along

the edge of a gully. When her nose
caught the scent of water, she knew
she was almost at Butterfly Brook.

Then, around a bend in the path,
Sophie saw it. A square of white

fabric stood out on the dark forest floor. She picked it up.

It was her handkerchief! The one she had given Winston for his knee! Now Sophie was sure. *He must have been here,* Sophie thought. *But . . . this isn't the way home.*

Then a completely new idea came to her.

What if Winston didn't go home at all?

chapter 9

Winston's Surprise

Sophie's mind was racing. But before she could make sense of it all, she heard a sound. It was slow and steady. *Knock, knock, knock.* She listened, then followed the sound.

The sound got louder as Sophie got closer to the source. *Knock . . . knock . . . knock . . .*

Sophie came over a little rise.

On the other side was a small gray mouse. He was holding a rock in one hand. He was using it like a hammer to pound a stick into the ground.

"WINSTON!" Sophie cried.

She ran to her brother. Winston stopped hammering. He looked up, startled, as Sophie plowed into him.

She swept him up in a huge hug.
Winston squirmed. But Sophie didn't
let go.

"Oh Winston, you have no idea
how glad I am to see you!"

"What are you doing?" Winston
asked when he was finally able to

wriggle free. "What's the big deal?"

Sophie sighed with relief. Then she began talking very fast. "Winston, I'm *so* sorry I sent you home before. But I went home looking for you. Because we needed your help. And you weren't at the house. Now I know it's because you never went there. Hey . . . but that means

you didn't listen to me! Never mind. I'm not mad. I've been searching everywhere for you. And here you are! I'm so glad you're okay!"

Winston looked confused for a second. He was taking it all in. "Of course I'm okay," he said. He put his hands on his hips. "But why did you need my help?"

Sophie smiled. She opened her mouth to tell him how he

could save the day with his knot-tying skills.

But before any words came out, Sophie noticed something. Behind Winston was a big structure. The stick that Winston had been hammering was part of it—just one small part.

Winston had built his own fort.
And it was an amazing fort!

Sophie gasped. "Winston, how
did you *do* this?" she
asked in wonder.

— chapter 10 —

Go, Team!

Winston smiled proudly. "You like it?" he asked Sophie.

Sophie nodded, speechless, as she studied the fort. Winston had used rocks as his building blocks. He had used wet mud to hold the rocks in place. This was how he had built up the walls. Then he had layered pine boughs on top to make the roof.

"I'm adding a front porch," said Winston. He picked up another stick. He hammered it into the ground with his rock.

"It's really, really cool," Sophie said, admiring it. "Can we show Hattie and Owen?"

Winston nodded. Sophie called

down toward the brook. "Hattie! Owen! Are you down there?"

Far off, Sophie heard their voices in reply. She called for them to come up. "You have to see this!" she shouted.

While they waited for Hattie and Owen, Sophie had an idea. But she wasn't sure what her brother would think of it.

"Um, Winston," she said timidly. "Do you need any

help? Because . . . I mean . . . if you *want*, we could help you finish your fort. We could build one giant fort together."

Winston stopped hammering.

"I don't *need* any help," he said.

Sophie's shoulders dropped. "Oh," she said sadly. "Okay. I understand if you want to do it yourself—"

Winston interrupted. "What I mean is, I *could* do it all by myself." He paused. "But if you *want* to help me, I guess you can. We could make a bigger and better fort if we worked together."

Sophie clapped in excitement. "Great!" she said. "It'll be so fun!"

Hattie and Owen came walking up. They were just as amazed by Winston's fort as Sophie was. And they hadn't gotten very far with their own fort, so they were happy to help Winston with his.

Winston worked on finishing the front porch. Owen and Hattie used Winston's extra rocks and mud to add another small room. Winston showed them how to tie the roof pieces together with super-strong knots! Sophie figured out how to put

a skylight in the roof. Then they all
worked together to add a front door.

When they were done, they found
rocks and bark pieces just the right

size for seats. They set them inside
the fort in a circle. Then they sat
down together. Sophie shared the
water and snacks she had in her
satchel.

494

"This is so cool!" said Winston. "Our own fort in the woods!"

"Wait until we tell Dad at dinner!" said Sophie. "He's going to be so proud of your building design, Winston!"

Sophie imagined painting a picture of her day after dinner. It would be a painting of their fort at Butterfly Brook. There would be blue morpho butterflies fluttering around. And her brother, Winston, would be right in the middle of the scene.

The End

Here's a peek at the next
Adventures of Sophie Mouse book!

Sophie Mouse tapped her pencil on her school desk. Her assignment was to write a math word-problem. Sophie wondered if Mrs. Wise would like hers.

Lily Mouse had 100 maple tarts to sell at the Maple Festival. She sold 20 before lunch. She sold 30 after lunch. How many did she have left to take home to her family?

Mmmm . . . thought Sophie as she reread the problem. Autumn was a very yummy time of year. It was when her mom made all kinds of maple treats at her bakery in Pine Needle Grove. And every year, Mrs. Mouse sold them at the big Maple Festival. Sophie couldn't wait for this

year's festival. It was coming up this weekend!

A cool breeze blew in through the window. It carried a few leaves with it.

"Okay, class!" Mrs. Wise called out. "Time for recess!"

The whole class jumped up. Sophie joined her friends Hattie Frog and Owen Snake at the door. They headed out to the playground.

"Are you both going to the Maple Festival this weekend?" Sophie asked them.

Hattie nodded. "Of course!" she said. "I want to ride the Ferris wheel at least five times!"

Owen gasped. "There will be a Ferris wheel?" His family had moved to Pine Needle Grove a few months before. He had never been to the Maple Festival.

"Owen, there's so much to do there!" Sophie cried. The three friends were nearing the swings. "There's dragonfly racing. You can play games to win prizes, like cranberry necklaces and acorn-top yo-yos!"

"There are ribbon-dancing grass-hoppers!" added Zoe, a bluebird who was swinging on a swing.

"And my mom's bake stand too!" added Winston, Sophie's little brother. He ran between Sophie and Hattie and was gone in a flash.

"Yummm," said several students, rubbing their bellies. Lily Mouse's bake stand was always one of the most popular attractions at the festival.

Ben, a rabbit who was Sophie's age, called out from the top of the slide. "I heard there's going to be a fire-breathing lizard this year!"

Sophie, Hattie, Owen, and Zoe looked at him in surprise.

Ben shrugged. "What?" he said. "That's what I heard!"

At home that evening, Sophie's mom and dad were talking about the festival too. "It's going to be a busy week," George Mouse said. He was an architect. Every year, he helped animals build their festival stands.

Lily Mouse looked more tired than usual. She had worked all day at the bakery. "Mrs. Fields isn't going to be able to help me this year. She is visiting friends in Briar Patch."

A chipmunk named Mrs. Fields

usually helped Lily Mouse the week before the festival. There was so much extra baking to do.

Sophie hurried over to her mom. "I can help you!" she offered. "I could be your assistant!"

Lily Mouse smoothed the fur on Sophie's head. "Thank you, Sophie," she said. "But I think I might need a grown-up to help me."

Sophie clasped her hands together. "Oh pleeeease, Mom," she pleaded. "You've always said that I'm a big help in the kitchen."

Lily Mouse looked at Sophie. She

seemed to be thinking it over.

Finally, she said, "Okay. We'll give it a try. You can start after school tomorrow."

Sophie cheered. Her mom smiled, but held up a hand.

"But don't say I didn't warn you," said Mrs. Mouse "There's a *lot* to do!"

Delicious Daydreams

After school the next day, Sophie dropped Winston off at his friend James's house for a playdate. Then

Sophie hurried toward the bakery. She was excited to be her mom's assistant for the Maple Festival!

Sophie ran through the village of Pine Needle Grove. Her nose picked up the sweet scent of maple sugar. Minutes later, she arrived at the bakery. She opened the front door.

"Hello?" Sophie called. There was no one up front.

Suddenly, there was a loud clatter from the kitchen. Sophie followed the sound. She pushed open the kitchen door. Her mom was standing in the middle of the room. At her feet was an overturned bowl and a puddle of batter.

"Oh dear," Lily Mouse cried. "I worked for *hours* on that maple cupcake batter." Her mom sighed.

Sophie patted her mom on the back. "I'll help you clean it up," she said. "Then we can mix up another batch."

Lily Mouse looked up at Sophie and smiled. "Thank you, sweetie," she said. "I've been rushing about all day. And I'm trying to come up with some new recipes for this year's festival. But I haven't thought of anything yet."

Sophie grabbed a mop. As she cleaned up the batter, she wondered if *she* could come up with a new recipe. *What would I invent if I were a baker?* Sophie thought. *What tastes good with maple? Daffodil petal? No. Too bitter. Pine cone dust? Nah. Too spicy.* Then Sophie stopped mopping. She had an idea!

"Mom," Sophie said, "how about a recipe that combines maple and apple?" Sophie thought it sounded perfect for autumn!

Lily Mouse was at the sink, washing the mixing bowl. She stopped

scrubbing. A smile slowly lit up her
face.

"Now why didn't I think of that?"
Lily Mouse said. "What a wonderful
idea, Sophie!"